This is the first novel of retired librarian J. M. Gidman. She was born in Yorkshire but has lived in Lancashire for a number of years. Her love of reading and history has led her to write two books and articles on historical subjects. She is a member of several local history societies and gives talks to local groups. Her first novel is a fusion of these interests and is the high point of her writing career. She is currently writing a sequel.

For John

Thanks for the Memories

J. M. Gidman

A QUESTION OF IDENTITY

AUSTIN MACAULEY PUBLISHERS™
LONDON • CAMBRIDGE • NEW YORK • SHARJAH

Copyright © J. M. Gidman (2021)

The right of J. M. Gidman to be identified as the author of this work has been asserted by the author in accordance with section 77 and 78 of the Copyright, Designs and Patents Act 1988.

All rights reserved. No part of this publication may be reproduced, stored in a retrieval system, or transmitted in any form or by any means, electronic, mechanical, photocopying, recording, or otherwise, without the prior permission of the publishers.

Any person who commits any unauthorized act in relation to this publication may be liable to criminal prosecution and civil claims for damages.

This is a work of fiction. Names, characters, businesses, places, events, locales, and incidents are either the products of the author's imagination or used in a fictitious manner. Any resemblance to actual persons, living or dead, or actual events is purely coincidental.

A CIP catalogue record for this title is available from the British Library.

ISBN 9781788230971 (Paperback)
ISBN 9781788231022 (ePub e-book)

www.austinmacauley.com

First Published (2021)
Austin Macauley Publishers Ltd
25 Canada Square
Canary Wharf
London
E14 5LQ

Chapter 1

For the umpteenth time that week, Sally Barton looked at the group of first-year students she was taking on the week's last introductory tour of the library.

It was September 2008 and during the first weeks of the Autumn Term, the senior library staff took parties of new students round the library explaining the layout, the arrangements for using the computer bank and the issue and loans policy. She sighed as she called the group of twenty or so around her. She looked at their faces. Some looked interested, some, rather more, looked bored and one or two even looked enthusiastic as though excited at the prospect.

"I'm going to have to watch those two," she thought. The eager ones always asked awkward questions.

Standing at the back of the group was a tall, thin man in his thirties, she thought, who could have been a mature student. He looked gravely at her as she began.

"Welcome to the Strickland Library of the University of South West Lancashire," she said for the last time that week. "My name is Sally Barton and I'm one of the Assistant Librarians. My job is mainly inter-library loans and I am also on the help desk, so if any of you need any help during your course just stop me and ask." This group were English students so she took them up to the third floor and showed them the English section, and then back down to the computers and the second floor and finally to the ground floor where the hub of the working and administrative area was. She demonstrated the catalogue and the issue and returns system and showed them where the Help Desk was. By this time all the students were looking bemused and when she asked if there were any questions even the enthusiastic students shrugged their shoulders as if anxious to get away to the bar.

"Well," she said, "I've given you a very brief taster of the library's facilities and where to ask for help if you get stuck, so good luck with your courses. You can collect your reader's ticket at the Help Desk on your way out."

The group dispersed and she gave a sigh of relief. It was all over for another year. But not quite. The tall young man was still standing nearby and as the students moved away, he approached her.

"My name is Ralph Armstrong," he said, "I'm a new lecturer in the English Department. I put in a request for books for my students and on checking the catalogue I find that they aren't listed."

"Ah well," answered Sally, "I think that you had better speak to Eileen Hanham, our Tutor Librarian who acts as academic liaison. As you will appreciate it can take some time for the system to settle down when new courses are started. I'm afraid that sometimes Libraries are a bit like the mills of God in that they work exceeding slow." Sally continued, "If you will just wait one moment I'll see if she is free."

Eileen was on the phone, so as they waited, she glanced at him and noted his thin, rather ascetic face, with its rather austere expression. His dress was the usual lecturer look of windcheater and jeans.

Sally explained, "There could be several reasons. For example, your list hasn't been sent through by the department or they decided to buy the books for the departmental library first and haven't sent the list through to us yet, but Eileen will be able to tell you what has happened. Ah! She's free now," she added as she saw that Eileen had finished her call.

She knocked on Eileen's door and as they entered the room, she said, "Eileen this is Mr Armstrong of the English Department."

"I'm very pleased to meet you, but actually, it's Dr Armstrong," he said as he shook hands.

Sally retreated rapidly from the doorway. Misquoting Longfellow to an English lecturer (what was she thinking) was one thing but getting his qualifications wrong was quite another. PhD's can be hypersensitive about their degree and notoriously touchy if you get their title wrong. "I won't be seeing him again," she thought.

She did not know how she made it back to the Workroom. As she went through the door, Pam Hawkins spotted her and made a beeline towards her.

"He looks just the type for you," she began, "good looking, tall, thin with just the right amount of gravitas."

"You must be joking," Sally replied. "I've just called him 'mister' and he's a 'Phud', and you know how particular they are about things like that."

"Oh, if he fancies you, all that will be forgotten," Pam ever the optimist shot back.

Sally, of all the senior staff, was the only one not married or in a relationship and Pam, happily married with two children, had decided that it was her mission in life to find Sally a man. Sally was not averse to this (as she always seemed to have trouble finding one herself) but was always a bit apprehensive about what Pam might say. Sally had visions of her going up to any likely prospect and telling him about her single friend. So far, she had not done it but Sally dreaded the day. At that moment Tracy, the Librarian's Secretary, came in with a sheaf of papers.

"Who's that gorgeous man talking to Eileen?" she said.

"Dr Armstrong," said Sally.

"Sally's new fella," said Pam.

"That was quick," commented Tracy.

"It's all in Pam's imagination," said Sally. "He's the new English lecturer and I've just got his title wrong and that will be that."

"Oh, you didn't!" exclaimed Tracy. She had done it once with a stickler and he had insisted on writing his complete qualifications list and underlining them on every message he sent across to the library. "I'm a PhD and don't you forget it," was the unspoken reprimand.

"I'm still going to keep him in mind for you," said Pam as she laughed and went back to work.

"Take no notice," said Tracy, "what will be, will be." Tracy could be very profound sometimes.

"Anyway," thought Sally, "it's all right choosing the fella but we know nothing about him. He could be married or in a relationship for all I know. He is rather fanciable though. For heaven's sake pull yourself together girl and get some work done," she told herself harshly, "daydreaming is all very well but real life is better." She went back to her inter-library loans.

Ralph Armstrong, meanwhile, and totally oblivious to the discussion as to his merits as a prospective partner for Sally, had finished his conversation with Eileen and now knew that the purchase of the books he had ordered was in hand. He had rather fancied Sally and had noticed the absence of rings on her left hand. He looked to see if she was about as he left the library but she was hidden somewhere in the back. As he walked back to his study he idly wondered if there was anyone serious in her life.

Over the next few weeks, Sally began to realise that whenever Dr Armstrong rang the library, she was getting the call. If she was on the Help Desk it wasn't a problem but eventually, she realised that, even when she wasn't on call, the staff were coming to look for her. At first, she did not realise that he was asking for her and thought that her colleagues, particularly Pam, wanted her to take the call, rather than them. She began to wonder if he was making fun of her, though why he should do so after one brief meeting she did not know.

Finally, after several weeks she was able to tell him that the books he had ordered were now catalogued and on the shelves. The next thing was an irate Dr Armstrong hurtling up to the Help Desk while she was on duty.

"Where are my books? You've told me they are on the shelves but I can't find them."

Sally was an essentially shy woman who disliked confrontation in any form. Normally she managed to put on a cool calm exterior professional manner to conceal this failing but under this circumstance, she blushed as she replied.

"I know they are on the shelves because I put them there myself."

"Well, they aren't there now."

"Let's go and have a look," said Sally calmly.

They went upstairs to the English Section. There on the shelf was the row of books that were causing all the trouble.

"But this isn't where I expected them to be," Armstrong exclaimed.

"Where did you expect them to be?" Sally asked.

"Over there in the 821s," he said.

"Ah, well here we put them at the end of the 823s," she explained.

"But I've told all my students to look over there."

"I'm sorry about that. Can you just alter the reading list? Better still let then find out from the catalogue."

"This is beginning to sound as though you are telling me my job."

He had spent several weeks asking firstly whether the books had been ordered, then whether they had arrived and finally when she had told him they were on the shelf this was his response. Sally was not going to let him get away with it.

"Heaven forbid! I would never dream of doing that," she replied with spirit, "but sometimes the lecturers seem to make their students' lives too easy!"

"Could you alter the class numbers to put the books where I want them?" he almost begged.

"We could but it would mean changing this lot as well, as they go together," she said, indicating half a shelf of titles. "It would be simpler to tell the students where they are."

"I can see that," he was beginning to calm down, "but why are they in a different place?"

"Do you want the short answer or the very long answer?" Sally was now firmly in charge of the situation.

"The short answer."

"The class number you wanted to use has already been used for another subject, and we already had some books on your subject which had been put over here."

"OK. What is the long answer?"

"It involves a minute dissection of the Dewey Decimal Classification system and takes several hours to explain."

"Why several hours?"

"Well, the odds are you would fall asleep in the middle and I would have to wait till you woke up before I could finish it. Then when I had finished, I would have to kill you," Sally said very seriously but with a twinkle in her eye, she was beginning to enjoy herself.

"Come again."

"I said, I would have to kill you."

"Why?"

"We have to protect our professional secrets," she said.

"How?"

"I beg your pardon."

"How would you kill me?" It was obvious he had caught the twinkle.

"That is entirely up to you. You have to pre-decide which way you want to go before we tell you."

"Ah, best stick to the short explanation then. I'll tell the students. However, if I ever feel that life's getting to be too much for me, or I start having trouble sleeping, can I book you for the long explanation?"

"Of course. My fees are very modest." She walked away.

"Must you always have the last word?" he sent a shouted whisper after her. She just turned, smiled, put her finger to her lips, nodded and winked.

While she walked away, she thought "Why do I always do that? I meet an attractive man and I seem to spend all my time putting my foot in it. Nerves I suppose. Why does everyone always think that I am in complete control? Relax, Sally, just enjoy life."

As she disappeared around the end on the shelving, Ralph thought "How did I get to meet a woman with such a great sense of humour, and get myself into such a ridiculous situation and make such an ass of myself. I walked into that one." And he gave a quiet laugh, which was not so quiet that Sally did not hear it.

When Sally got back to the Help Desk, Pam was hovering.

"Where have you been?" she asked, "I've got some great news for you."

"I've been sorting Dr Armstrong out," replied Sally. "Go on, what's the news?"

"Well, it's about him," said Pam. "I knew you were made for each other. He went to Leeds University. You've got that in common."

"Oh, come on!" exclaimed Sally. "I don't think you can base a relationship on that."

"Well, it's something. Stranger things have happened," Pam finished mysteriously as she disappeared back into the Workroom.

"I do wish people would leave me alone to make my own messes," thought Sally as she got back to work.

That evening as Sally left the campus, Ralph was pulling out of the driveway in his car. He saw her walking and braked slightly thinking he would offer her a lift. However, fearful of a refusal, he tooted his horn and gave a wave as he drove passed and out into the main road.

Sally returned his wave and walked on. As she walked, she pondered on the week and thought about what she needed to do and what she wanted to do during the weekend. Her Friday evening walk home had become part of her routine. During it, she sorted her life out. Her plans for the following week and her immediate plans for the weekend. Ormsbury, where the University of South West Lancashire was situated, had only the university as its main employer in the district. As a result, she had learnt long ago that the best way to settle into a new place was to take part in local activities. Many local people worked at the university but the majority of the academic staff had come in from outside and this was how she had come there. Although not a member of the teaching staff she had responded to an advertisement in the professional press for applicants for an Assistant Librarian post. In this, she had been successful coming from a year of getting her library qualifications following her Open University Degree and her work as a library assistant at Leeds University. Since coming to Ormsbury she had joined the local Amateur Operatic Society as she enjoyed singing and also the Family History Society as she wanted to trace her family now that she was on her own. The latter Society had jumped at the opportunity of having a professional librarian to run their library and she had been glad to get involved.

Her walk took her down the slight slope towards the town to the west and by this time of the year the sun was getting low in the sky and silhouetting the church on its rock in the middle of town. It was much stunted now from what it had been in its heyday as a centre of pilgrimage to the tomb of the Norse Saint Orm. Henry VIII had a lot to answer for. The tomb of the saint had been long lost under what had once been the chancel floor. Now all that remained of the original church was the nave which had been converted into the parish church. Its tower still stood, stark against the early autumnal sky.

She hated the walk. West Lancashire was too flat for her. She vastly preferred a few hills, or even the odd bump or two, but all around was flat out to the west and the Irish Sea at Southport. Not as vast as Norfolk but just as flat.

So this weekend she decided that she had better go down to the Family History Library and find out what needed doing and then after she had done that, she could look at the music for the Operatic Society's next production. A bit old fashioned now but fun to do, Gilbert and Sullivan's 'The Mikado' had been chosen. Not a bad weekend. Dull, but restful, after a hectic week at work.

For the rest of the term Ralph Armstrong managed to keep out of Sally's way and she, in turn, was grateful that she had no opportunity to make a fool of herself. Ralph was a man on a mission and getting involved at this stage in his life, here, in this place now, was not part of it. When he had completed his task, he would see how things were then. However, he had taken to sitting in the magazine section of the library and reading the daily newspapers. As a result, he had seen Sally at work and saw how she dealt with enquiries and realised that she was a very hands-on person.

The first time this happened it was by accident. He had gone to check a news story and Sally had walked through with one of the readers in order to show them the reference material needed to answer their query. He liked this approach, which was essentially a teaching situation, and saw that it was appreciated by the readers and began to realise that the humour Sally injected into her work was part of her personality. He also recognised that while she took her job seriously, she did not take herself too seriously. He found that he was beginning to look for this lively person of about 5ft 6ins in height with dark wavy hair and dancing hazel eyes.

Chapter 2

Sally did not see much of Ralph Armstrong for the rest of the term. She occasionally saw him in passing both in the main building, in the Senior Common Room, and of course in the library but, as there was no reason to talk, a smile and a greeting was all that was necessary. By this time she was beginning to really like the look of him and did wonder a little more about him. Pam had told her that he was not married and as far as she could find out was not currently in a relationship. Sally thought that Ralph rather liked her as his greetings were always warm but he never stopped to even pass the time of day with her and so thought that she was not his type and did not start chasing him. Sally Barton did not chase men. Perhaps she should do, but her father, the dear thing, had said that that was a definite no-no and she always did what her father said in these matters, or nearly always.

Ralph Armstrong, on the other hand, looked forward to these unexpected meetings and occasionally wandered into the Senior Common Room more than once a day to check his mail in the hope of catching a glimpse of her. He had applied for the post at West Lancashire University with a purpose, and it was only for two years and in that time, he hoped to solve his family mystery. To do this he needed to get to know the area and find people who might be able to help. There would, he hoped, be plenty of time to get to know Sally better when his task was underway.

The Staff Christmas party was one of the social highlights of the university year. The university was so vast that members of one department had little opportunity to get to know, or mix with, members of another and so it was an opportunity for them to get together for a buffet and a dance. This year Jim Potter, one of the English staff, who was interested in drama (as opposed to a member of the drama staff who was interested in parties), had organised an entertainment, which consisted of a revue-style look at incidents that had occurred during the academic year. Sally, following her interest in drama, had joined when Jim had first suggested a staff drama group. She had been given a small part which involved dressing all in black, including black tights, which said rather more about the director of the performance than the entertainment itself.

The night of the Christmas social was on Friday the last night of term when the resident students had, mostly, left for the break, so the staff could let their hair down. Sally had been relieved to find that Dr Armstrong had not got involved in the entertainment and so had only her acting nerves to overcome. The evening began with the entertainment which was followed by the buffet and dancing. It was not until after she had performed her satirical number that she realised he had come to see the fun. He had been sitting at the back of the hall and came up to congratulate her on her performance. He had come with several members of his department and re-joined them for the buffet. Sally joined the group from the library and the evening progressed.

After the buffet, the dancing started. A band had been brought in which consisted of a member of staff and his Jazz combo. At first, couples danced and then members of the various groups. As always at these events departments tended to stay together with very little cross-fertilisation between them. Sally had no partner so only danced the disco dances with her friends. A quickstep was announced and she found someone standing in front of her. She looked up and it was Dr Armstrong.

"Would you like to dance this?" he asked.

"Yes, I'll have a go," she said, "but I've never danced the quickstep before."

"If you're game then I am," he replied. "Just hold on tight and follow me." They stood up as the music started. He held her close, her head came just above his shoulder, and it felt good. He was a good dancer, who knew what he was doing, and all Sally had to do was follow him. She was a quick learner and soon picked up the basic steps, though she did feel as though she was hanging on like grim death. Halfway through, he decided to up the pace, and after whispering "Hold on tight", he proceeded to double the speed and they shot across the floor as if there was no stopping them. They swung and swayed, turned and sashayed until the music stopped and Sally was left breathless.

As he took her back to her seat he said, "Can I have the last word this time?"

She looked at him with dancing eyes having thoroughly enjoyed herself but could only nod.

Her companions said, "What on earth was all that about?" Sally was totally bemused.

Ralph had enjoyed the dance, his mother's insistence on the dancing lessons all those years ago had finally paid off. Besides, he had realised that he really was attracted to Sally but knew that he wanted to solve his mystery before getting involved with anyone. His previous girlfriends had not been sympathetic and he wanted to know the answer and lay it to rest before, getting involved again. But the look of delight on Sally's face as he walked her off the floor made him wonder if he wasn't making a big mistake. He had almost kissed her, there and then, in front of everybody but stopped himself just in time. This was neither the time nor the place for that.

The rest of the evening passed in a blur for Sally but all too soon it was ending and time for home. Sally had a lift from Pam and her husband Richard and Pam quizzed her all the way home about Ralph Armstrong.

"I told you he liked you," she said.

"I know you did," Sally replied, "but nothing goes any further. I see him about the library and he always says 'Hello' but no hint of a drink or 'Can I join you in a sandwich?' So I think he must have other fish to fry."

"Don't give up hope," counselled Pam.

"Oh, you two, give the poor man a chance. You'd have him down the aisle before breakfast if you had your way, Pam." Richard was used to Pam's matchmaking activities which always depressed him a little as it usually meant another good man gone west.

"Thanks, Richard," said Sally. "If he likes me, it'll happen; if not, I'm not going to let it get me down. I like him but liking is not enough. Can we give it a rest for now?"

"All right, I won't say any more, but I won't stop hoping," said Pam. "I think that he's just right for you."

They dropped Sally off at her little house and she was glad to put the day and evening behind her as she closed the front door. But as she was falling asleep that night the dance tune ran through her head and she felt again Ralph Armstrong holding her and she admitted to herself that she had enjoyed herself very much and hoped that he liked her and that next term something might happen.

Sally was due to go south to her brother, Les's, for Christmas if the weather was good enough. But there was another week to go before she set off. Monday was a workday. She took Monday afternoon off to go to Family History to see the rest of the committee and make sure everyone was happy with the library there.

Ralph left after the weekend to go home for the holiday.
They did not meet again until the beginning of the next term.

Chapter 3

By the beginning of the Spring Term Ralph had begun to understand and appreciated the dynamics of the English Department. He understood that Mary Johnstone, a formidable woman in her late fifties and heading for retirement, the 'mother', of the Department and oldest resident, was a suffragette of the old school whose opinion of men was that they were slightly higher in the order of evolution to an amoeba. However, she did not let it interfere in her day-to-day relationships with her colleagues. Her main bone of contention was that a man had been brought in over her head to be Head of Department when the previous occupant, a woman, and close friend of Mary's, had retired. She had been once heard to remark in the context of mature students, 'My dears, have you ever met a mature male'. This, essentially, was beside the point as Ralph soon discovered that she knew everybody who was anybody in the department and university. As a result, when he finally came to the conclusion that, having now been there for a whole term, he should now start trying to find out the answer to his mystery, it was to Mary that he turned to ask for the name of someone to help.

"Mary," he began, "I am looking for some assistance in doing some research for me, nothing to do with my course work but a private matter. Can you suggest someone who might both help and be discreet?"

She looked at him. "I presume that this needs to be someone with research skills as well as discretion?" she said.

"Well, yes," he replied. Mary did always seem to wrong-foot him.

"And this matter is of a private and confidential nature?" she said thoughtfully

"Yes."

"In that case, I think you could do worse than ask Sally Barton in the library. She is noted for her infinite resource, sagacity, and discretion. She actually knows where all the bodies are buried but never says," was Mary's conclusion.

At this Ralph's heart rose. He had been hoping to find a good excuse to talk to Sally again but then he remembered and his heart sank. He had already made a fool of himself in front of Sally and was not looking forward to doing it again.

"Don't look so worried," Mary said. "I understand you and she got on famously at the Christmas party. I don't go to such things. They are intended to foster social intercourse with a view to perpetuating the species and I have never been entirely convinced that the male of the species needs perpetuating. However, I do hear of the goings-on at these events and I suppose I really cannot stop others from enjoying themselves. But if you want help, Sally is your girl."

Once term started again after Christmas Sally had been kept busy in the library but on one Thursday morning early in February, she was at her timetabled station on the Help Desk when Dr Ralph Armstrong came to her. He looked about to make sure he wasn't overheard and Sally was intrigued by this. Most inquiries were almost always shouted to the housetops on the 'look what I am interested in' principle.

"Excuse me, er, Sally," he said. His approach was rather diffident.

She looked at him expectantly. Who knew what exciting request might be coming. "Yes? Can I help you?"

"Mary Johnstone, in my department, said that you might be able to help me."

"I know Mary."

"Well, she said that you were a person of infinite resource, sagacity and discretion."

"That sounds like Mary. I'm not sure that it's me though."

"I have a query of a personal nature that I wouldn't want generally known."

Now definitely intrigued Sally looked all ears. "You mean it isn't something you can discuss in public."

"Something like that."

"Well if you want a quiet chat then Friday afternoon tea break in the Senior Common Room is your best bet. Hardly anybody is in there then. Would you like to meet there tomorrow afternoon?"

"OK. I'll see you there then." He left the library hastily.

Pam, who had caught the end of the conversation, said, "What on earth was all that about? We can't have the dishiest man in the place coming in and making assignations in the library."

"Oh, shut up. It's probably something for his own private work and he wants to sit on it till he knows if it's any good."

The next afternoon Sally was already having her cup of tea when Dr Armstrong appeared. As promised no one else was there.

"I'm sorry that I haven't got long as I have to be back in the library in another ten minutes. I'm afraid my breaks are timetabled," she said.

"I'll be as quick as I can. It's rather personal, by that I mean, it relates to my family not directly to me. My family originally comes from here that is Ormsbury, and my grandfather left when my father was a baby and we have always been told we should not come back. I want to know why. Can you help?"

"Well, I can try. But I will need as much information as you have."

"That isn't much."

"Are there names, dates etc. that could help? Look time is running on. Why don't you come for coffee to my place tomorrow and tell me all about it?"

"Are you sure you don't mind doing this?"

"It sounds interesting. I'll help you all I can but I can't promise anything."

"What time tomorrow?"

"Make it about eleven," and she gave him her address. "Bring any info you've got."

Chapter 4

The next morning at eleven promptly the doorbell rang and Dr Armstrong was standing on the doorstep holding a bottle of wine and a very slim folder.

Sally's compact, two bedroomed, terraced house was situated on a busy street which led off the Market Place along which traffic headed out of town. She had applied for and been given the post of Assistant Librarian in Ormsbury before her parents had died. Their sudden death in a car accident on the M1 had thrown all her plans out of the window. They had left everything to be divided between Les and herself and she had been able to afford this little house out of her share.

Her front door opened onto the footpath. Inside there was a short passage. The stairs rose at right angles between the front and back rooms. The front room was small and faced north and did not get any sun so Sally preferred to be at the back. However, that did not stop her using it to keep some of her vast collection of books and some pieces of furniture that had belonged to her parents which she was loath to get rid of.

The backroom, where Sally spent most of her time, extended the full width of the house. There was a fireplace on the sidewall, at the right hand of which, and under the stairs in an alcove, was a desk with a laptop computer on it. Against the outer wall, under the window, was a small dining table. Just inside from the hall was a large settee. Everywhere there were bookcases crammed with books. The kitchen led out of the living room and extended into the sunny back yard. Beyond the yard, an access road had been put in with garages.

Sally took Ralph through to the living room, where it was possible to lay out material on the small dining table.

"Coffee, tea or cocoa, Dr Armstrong?" she asked.

"Tea preferably," he replied. "Please call me Ralph."

"OK, Ralph, I know it's all first names at work but I wasn't sure you had forgiven me for getting it wrong last term."

"Don't be daft, and I'm afraid I don't drink coffee, too much caffeine."

"That's OK," she said, "everyone invites you for coffee but I don't drink it either." She went into the tiny kitchen and switched on the kettle, put a teabag in a mug and hot chocolate in the other mug and came back into the living room. "Do you want to drink first before looking at your papers, on the principle that if we put them out something will get spilt on them?"

"Good idea." So they sat at the table.

"What made you come here?" she asked.

"I wanted to get this mystery solved before I could get on with my life," he said.

"That's pretty drastic," Sally commented. At that point, the kettle boiled and she got up to make the drinks. She brought them back to the table and sat down.

"I forgot to ask if you take milk or sugar," she said. "I'm always doing that."

"Both," was the reply so she went back to get them and sat down again.

"Help yourself."

"I think that there is something I should warn you about before searching for your ancestors. It applies to anyone who starts looking into the past. You've got to have an open mind and be prepared to find out anything. Sometimes it can be something that perhaps you would rather not have known about. Remember the past is the past. While finding out about our ancestors can change our perception of them it can't actually hurt us. Sorry about that, sermon over. I just wanted you to know what you might be getting into. Is that OK? Do you want to carry on?"

Ralph pondered for a few moments and came to a decision. "Yes," he said, "I've wanted to know. So here goes. Carry on Sally."

"Can you tell me about it or is it confidential?" Sally asked. "If you would rather not tell me I will have to ask questions, I hope you realise that. It's not possible to do this blind."

"I realise that, but I did not want to discuss it at work because it could be iffy."

"OK. Tell me what you can."

"As I understand it my grandfather had to leave Ormsbury about sixty years ago. He took my grandmother and my father who was about four years old at the time and left. They went over to Yorkshire and lived in Cleckheaton, where I come from until they died. Grandfather died when my father was about twelve and his mother died about twelve years ago. Dad died eight years ago and I could not find any papers. There was no birth certificate for my father only his marriage certificate and Mum could tell me nothing when I went to register the death. All of his details had to be estimated."

"Why do you think they came from here?"

"Dad talked about it sometimes, saying that he could not understand why it was so important that nobody should know where he came from, and that I mustn't tell anyone. I mean it did not bother me when I was younger, at school, I was local and that was all that mattered – but now, after his death, it seems important."

"Can't your mother help?"

"She knew nothing. Dad never talked about it. She never knew his father and apparently, grandmother would say nothing. When asked all she would say was, "What you don't know can't hurt you." I was away at Oxford when she died so missed out on any family confab. I only made it home for the funeral. Besides Mum died about six months after Dad so when this job came up, I jumped at it. There is however one problem, my sister Gloria, although she prefers to be called Ria, does not want me looking into this. I think she's a bit frightened of what I might find out."

"So you're an orphan too. You'll have to come to the orphans' picnic." Why did she always say the wrong thing, but Ralph did not seem to notice so she continued, "Just so you know a little about me. I too come from Yorkshire, Leeds this time. I came about six years ago when the job at the library became vacant. My parents have died since but I have a brother, Les, Leslie, who is in the forces and is based away. I see him sometimes and his family. In fact, I went for Christmas. Lancashire is not bad to live in once you get used to the sense of humour; it's a bit different from home. Perhaps I meet it more as most of the people I work with are local whereas most of the academic staff come from elsewhere. Now then let's have a look at this paperwork."

Together, they cleared the table and spread the meagre array of papers out.

"This is my parents' marriage certificate, my father's death certificate, and my mother's death certificate but we shouldn't need that and my grandmother's death certificate. I'm afraid that's it," said Ralph as he laid them out.

"This is a little strange. There's no death certificate for your grandfather. No matter. There should also be a birth certificate for your father as he would probably have needed it when he got married. So what happened to it? Anyway, it isn't here so we'll try and work around it. How old was your father when he died? I see he was fifty-six. Right, you think he was born here so if we look at the free births, marriages and deaths website we might find his birth."

Sally went across to her computer which was sitting in the alcove next to the fireplace and switched it on. As it was warming up, she asked, "When was your father's birthday?"

"30 May."

"So if we look in the June quarter for 52 years ago, we should find it then. So we are looking for John Armstrong." She said as she checked the marriage certificate.

She entered the details into the website and got no hits. She tried again for the next quarter again without any results. "Let's try a year earlier. Nothing. A year later. Mmm, nothing. I'll put in a five-year search. Nothing. Ten years. Nothing. This is odd. If it was a woman and I was looking for a death you might assume that she had remarried. But a man is different they don't usually change their names. Perhaps that's it, their name was changed."

"You mean I'm not really an Armstrong?"

"Could be. Can you live with that? Look don't despair." She put a comforting hand on his arm. "There could be several reasons for this," Sally said encouragingly. "I think the best thing I can do is go to the Public Library and use their system to get into BMDs and check the pages. The other thing I can do is go to check the baptism registers for the local churches and see if anything comes up. If the surname was changed then the Christian names could be the same and it might be possible to get them that way. Also, it might just be a spelling error. Leave it with me and I'll see what I can do. What were your grandparents' Christian names?"

"George and Betty, at least that's what we always called them. Look, I don't want you to be out of pocket on this, let me know what I owe you."

"No problem. This means we are going to have to keep in touch. You know what this place is like, both the town and the Uni. Gossip shops both. Unless you want this on the grapevine it might be best to play it cool."

"There's no one to bother about me if it's OK with you."

"Let's see how it goes."

Chapter 5

Sally's timetable at the library meant that one evening a week she was on duty until 9.00 pm with the morning of that day off, so she started work at 1.00 pm. This enabled her to spend one morning doing what she wanted at a time when other institutions were open. As a result, she was able to spend Monday morning in the Public Library using their internet facilities to look up anything she wanted. In this way, she spent time looking for birth for John Armstrong with reference to the town. As she had discovered from the free service there was no reference in the appropriate quarter, she checked at the adjacent quarters without luck and then, working from the assumption that the family had not changed their initials even though they may have changed their name she began to note all the A's born in the town during the relevant quarter. It was a slow and tedious business but she made steady progress.

Each week she continued from where she had left off the previous week and each Saturday morning Ralph came round for a cup of tea to see if any progress had been made. As progress was slow these turned into social get-togethers and Sally began to wonder where this was leading.

Towards the end of the Spring Term on a Saturday morning, Ralph came round, and over a cup of tea, they looked at the material that Sally had found. It did not amount to much. By this time she had worked her way through the June Quarter and into the September Quarter but tracking down each reference to a 'John' would prove rather expensive if all the certificates were sent for.

"Term ends next week," said Ralph, "and I'm going over to Cleckheaton. My tenants have left and I want to see what state the house is in. Would you like to come too?"

"Actually I was going to ask if you minded me going over anyway because I thought of looking for your grandparents grave. It might give some clues," Sally replied.

"How do you mean?"

"I can't trace any Armstrongs at this end. I thought that if I looked on the ground there might be a bit of additional information that might have been missed. Were they buried or cremated? I know you said you were at your grandmother's funeral was at in the crematorium or in a cemetery? Can you remember if there was a stone?"

"Let me think. Yes, there was a burial and I seem to remember seeing a stone. But it was so long ago, I may have got it wrong."

"Right, well if it is all right with you, I'll come and have a look."

"I was planning to go next week."

"A weekday would be best because if we need to check anything, we need to be there during office hours."

"What about Tuesday?"

"I'll see if I can take it off."

Ralph leant back in his chair. "You know I do like your little house."

"I beg your pardon."

"I mean you've made it into a home."

"That's what we women do you know, despite what the feminists say, we have this knack."

"I know, but somehow this feels like a home. Who did your decorating?"

"I did."

"I thought so, you've missed a bit."

"I know. Where?"

"Up there." He indicated a corner at the top of the wall.

"I didn't, not there. You're making this all up. I know I missed a bit but only I know where."

"Actually I can't see a missed bit. It's an old decorator's joke. My father was a painter and decorator, and when I was helping him at home, he always used to say that to me. It used to drive me wild. This is the first time I've ever used it on someone else."

"Thank you so very much," she said sarcastically. "As far as me making this into a home, I think you've been living out of cardboard boxes too long."

"You're probably right. Damn! You've had the last word again!"

"I was wondering why you came around so often. Now I know it's my house you're after."

"Not only the house."

"Now who's had the last word?"

Chapter 6

Early the following Tuesday Ralph picked Sally up in his large roomy car, needed to contain his lanky frame, and they set off along the motorway to Yorkshire.

They drove out of Ormsbury toward the M6 to head south towards the M62.

"You prefer the M6/M62 route, do you?" said Sally when they were well on their way.

"Yes, is there another?" replied Ralph.

"I usually go along the East Lancs Road, it's got more hazards and keeps me awake."

"I see your point, but just sit back and enjoy, and let me worry about keeping awake."

After a while, Ralph said, for no apparent reason, "You don't drink do you?"

"Not really, alcohol doesn't agree with me. Why?"

"I was just thinking, we've known each other a while now and not once have you tried to get me drunk and have your wicked way with me."

Sally looked at him astounded. Then she saw the beginning of a smile around the corners of his mouth.

"Hmm," she thought, "I'm not going to let him get away with that." She said, "Do you think that your reputation has preceded you to the extent that all the girls are trying to get you into bed then?"

"Well you haven't given me much indication as to whether you like me or not."

"You've not asked me out yet so I wasn't going to say anything until you did. My dear old Dad always said, 'Let the fellow make the first move, you don't want to frighten him off.'"

"Well, we're going out now."

"Yes, but this isn't a date."

"Isn't it. I thought you might turn down the usual 'Come and have a drink line', so I've had to get really creative to get you out today."

"This isn't a date. It's a working holiday. Besides which I asked if I could come so that doesn't count. Besides are you such a catch that I should have wanted to get you drunk and have my wicked way?"

"I've had no complaints," he said.

"Well neither have I," Sally replied. "I didn't need to get them drunk either."

"I bet you didn't."

"I think sex stone cold sober is much more fun that a drunken fumble. Besides, you can remember how it was the next day not spent days wondering what happened."

"You've got a point there."

"Oh!" Sally exclaimed as they reached to the foot of the Pennines just outside Milnrow. "This is my favourite bit of the journey. We've reached the Pennines and Yorkshire's just up there."

"Mine too. When I get here, I know that I'll be home soon."

The road wound up the hillside and under the footbridge that takes the Pennine Way across the motorway. At the top, the hills the upland moorland of Saddleworth Moor widened out with a broad prospect of the Booth Wood Reservoir below them so close that they could almost touch it and see the water lapping over the dam driven by the wind. In the distance on one side was Halifax shrouded in haze and on passed Scammonden Water, formed when the dam was built with the motorway on top. Then along to the gap in the hills through which could be glimpsed Huddersfield in the valley below. The sun shone; it was a beautiful day. Soon they went past Hartshead Moor Services and turned down into Cleckheaton. Sally had never been here before despite going passed it many times on her way back to Leeds.

As they went down the slip road and into Cleckheaton Ralph said, "Thank you for your chatter, I was beginning to get a bit worried about what we might find out when we got here. So I talked nonsense."

"So did I."

"I've been thinking about what you said regarding the change of name. You shook me for a moment. I had not thought of that. You said at the beginning that I might not like what you found out, but I wasn't expecting that."

"That's only one possibility but it might explain why we haven't found anything so far. But again keep an open mind. If the truth can set us free, then we can take it as far as you want to go."

It was about 10.00 am when they arrived in Cleckheaton and drove back over the M62 to Cleckheaton New Cemetery in Scholes where Ralph remembered his grandmother's funeral taking place. One look at the expanse of graves told them they would need help finding it.

At the cemetery office, they asked the rather taciturn cemetery keeper where the grave of Elizabeth Armstrong was. In return they were asked when she died and had the grave been used before. After a lot of discussions and a look on the computer (fortunately the index to graves had been computerised for the last ten years), there was the hope of locating it. Two Elizabeth Armstrongs had been buried in that time and armed with the plot numbers they went to look. The first grave had only one name on it although the date was about right, the second had the stone they were looking for.

In Loving Memory of George, A Armstrong died 4 September 1962 aged 32. A Good Husband and Father. Also Elizabeth his wife died 19 January 1996 Together.

"You didn't tell me your grandfather had a middle name," Sally said.

"I didn't know," Ralph replied. "Is that a clue?"

"Could be. We'll have to see the burial entry in the book now we have the plot number."

Sally took a photograph of the stone before they went back to the office together. The keeper was in no better mood. He was obviously having a bad day.

"We've found the right grave but would like to look at the burial register. How would we go about doing that?" Sally asked.

"When was the burial?" the keeper brusquely asked.

"In 1962," she replied.

"If you want to go as far back as that you'll have to go to the Record Office. The old burials books have gone there. As long as you have the plot number and the name of the Cemetery you should be able to find it."

"Where's the Record Office?" Ralph asked.

"In Bradford, since the reorganization," they were told.

They came out of the office dispirited. Bradford was in the opposite direction from where Ralph wanted to be and they only had the one car.

"I should have come in my car," said Sally, "then we could have split up. Look, if I get a bus into Bradford can you do what you want and pick me up later or shall I get a bus back and meet you here?"

"You've given me the bug. I'm coming too. I want to know all about this. I can come back to check on the house later. This is more important."

They drove into Bradford, located the Record Office and found a parking space. By this time, it was long past lunchtime.

"Do you want something to eat?" Ralph asked.

"Let's grab a sandwich and go straight there," Sally replied. Which is what they did.

Inside the Record Office, they explained what they wanted and had to produce forms of identification; fortunately, Sally had her Lancashire Record Office reader's card which helped and Ralph had a driving licence. They were directed to the index and after a lot of argument located the index number for the burials book. They then had to put in a request and wait patiently for 20 minutes until it was brought. Waiting was not easy. Both were in a high state of anticipation of what it might reveal.

When the volume came, they, carefully, opened it together and looked for the plot number and the date. There it was:

The burial of *"George Ashcroft, aged 32, 26 Slater Street, Cleckheaton. 10 September 1962."*

"That's him," said Sally.

"But it says Ashcroft, not Armstrong," protested Ralph. "And it says Armstrong on the stone."

"They changed their name," said Sally. "Your grandmother pulled a flanker. She buried him as Ashcroft but put A Armstrong on the stone. It was genius. No one would find him."

An attendant came over. "Please can you keep the noise down?"

"Sorry. Is it possible to make a copy of this entry?" Sally asked.

"You may take photographs for a fee of £5.00 but we do not do photocopying."

Sally paid £5.00 and took the photograph. As they went outside, Ralph suddenly slumped.

"I thought I would be elated when I found out something and now it has thrown all my ideas out of the window. I'm not who I thought I was."

"Yes, you are. The fact that there has been a name change alters nothing. You are still Ralph Armstrong, that's the name you were given when you were born and your genes have not altered you are who you always have been." Sally was very firm on this. "Besides," she added with a twinkle, "as a well-known man from Warwickshire once said, 'A rose by any other name…'"

He walked up and down for a while and Sally leant against the side of the building.

"You're right. Nothing has really changed, has it? I am lucky to have you on my side in this quest." He put his arm around her and kissed her. "Thank you," he said.

He grabbed her hand and hurried off towards the car park.

"Where are we going?" Sally said.

"Back to Cleckheaton," he replied. But as they hurried, she realised that there was something wrong. He appeared to be having some kind of crisis. She dragged him into a café and ordered a pot of tea for four.

When it came, she poured him a strong cup and put plenty of sugar in it and then poured herself one.

"Here drink this," she said. "You've had a shock. I think you need this."

"What the hell's happening to me?" he said.

"Your world's just turned around. It'll settle down shortly." 'Or longly,' she thought.

When he had drunk his tea and appeared a little calmer, she again asked what he wanted to do next.

"Go back home to Cleckheaton," he replied.

"Well, you're in no fit state to drive so will you let me?" and he gave her the keys.

Together they made their way back to the car park and Sally drove back toward Cleckheaton. Ralph sat slumped in the passenger seat of the car and said nothing until they reached the edge of the town when Sally said, "Can you direct me?" and he directed her to the house where he used to live.

It was a neat little house in a terrace, with a small garden at the front with a bay window jutting out into it. These houses were the next step up from the terraces which front onto the street and have no bay windows. Mr & Mrs Armstrong had done their best.

"Here we are," Sally said, as she drew up outside.

Ralph fumbled for the key and Sally gently took it from him and inserted in the lock. Ralph turned it and they went into the little hall. The house was similar to Sally's in Ormsbury but was slightly bigger and the layout was not quite the same. Because it was set back from the street the front door opened directly into the front room and the backroom opened out of it and beyond that was the kitchen. The stairs were directly opposite the front door rising from the tiny hall with a door into the living room, and there was a right-angled turn near the top. There was a little garden at the back with what had been flowerbeds or a vegetable patch. Unlike Sally's house, there was no drying ground, and consequently nowhere to garage a car, which therefore had to be parked on the quiet street outside.

As they moved through the house, they could see that the tenants had left a bit of a mess. Everywhere smelt stale, as though it had not been lived in for a while, which was odd because the tenants had only just moved out. Bits of paper were left strewn on the floor but the kitchen was tidy. The mess was not great, so it would take only a short time to get it ready for a new tenant. With a sigh, Ralph sat on the floor of the front room and leant against the wall.

After a while, he said, "I'm sorry I've got you into this."

Sally sat down beside him and took his hand.

"You haven't got me into anything," she replied. "I knew when we started this…er quest, that you might find out things that you would rather not know, and if you remember I did warn you, but there's no forecasting how you are going to feel about them when you do find out."

"Are you saying, 'I told you so'?"

"No, I'm not. I'm just reminding you, that's all. It can stop here. There's no need to find out anymore if you don't want to."

"My head tells me that you're making sense but I can't seem to stop shaking."

"That's the shock. It'll wear off eventually when it all makes sense. It just seems to have hit you harder than most."

"I've got this incredible urge to discuss it with Dad and of course he's not here anymore."

"I know. Perhaps you started on this too soon after he died."

"Maybe so. What do we do now?"

"You came to look at the house. It was my idea to go to the cemetery. So that part of the day is my fault, and I'll do anything I can to help. Let's have a proper look round the house and see what needs to be done and then take it from there."

"You mean be practical."

"Yes. Activity will help."

"Is this how you cope?"

"What makes you think I can cope? Sometimes the surface may seem smooth, but like the ducks, or do I mean swans, I am paddling away like mad below the waterline."

She pulled him from the floor and together they examined the state of the house.

"A couple of hours should see it tidy," Ralph said. He went outside and opened the boot of the car and brought out a bucket and mop, a sweeping brush and dustpan, and a roll of disposable cloths. He also produced a kettle. "That's for hot water," he said.

By the time they had finished it was getting late.

"I did not expect you to help with the cleaning," he said to Sally.

"I know," she said, "but I'm not leaving you until you feel better."

"Thanks," he replied, "Let's go and find something to eat."

Chapter 7

They were just thinking about locking up the house when a whirlwind erupted. A woman in her forties burst through the front door and found them sitting on the floor in the front room.

"When were you going to come and see me?" She demanded.

Ralph looked up. "Hello Sis," he said. And to Sally, "This is my sister Ria."

Ria looked at Sally. "Is this one of your bimbos?" she asked.

"No, this is my friend Sally who is helping me with a project," he replied getting up from the floor. He looked really tired and washed out and Sally could see that he was not looking forward to this confrontation.

"I think we had better go and discuss our private affairs in the kitchen, don't you?" he said, leading the way towards the back of the house.

Sally went to sit on the stairs out of the way and closed the door into the front room. Sally could still hear the voices despite the closed door although it masked a lot of the sound. She looked through the photographs of the gravestone, and the burial record from the Record Office, which were on her camera; she took out her notebook and searched in her bag for a pencil and made a few notes. Then, spying her unread newspaper in her bag she took it out and read for a while. She then began to do the crossword puzzle as the voices droned on.

The voices went on and on. Ria's tending to be rather shrill at times meant that her words could be overheard.

"What were you doing in the cemetery?" Ria demanded. "Don't try to deny it you were seen."

"I was showing Sally a gravestone she was particularly interested in," he said.

"Rubbish," countered Ria, "You're trying to solve the family mystery. When will you learn that no good can come of it? Dad didn't want us to find out, and neither do I. Now you've gone to live in Ormsbury and he told us not to, God knows what trouble you'll stir up."

"That's why I have gone. Look, Sally isn't local, in fact, she comes from the other side of Leeds, towards York, so anything we find out will stay between us. It will cut down any fallout. As I get older it seems to have taken quite a hold of me. We are going to solve the riddle whether you like it or not. Whatever I find I'll keep to myself if you would prefer it that way. But I am going to find out."

"What if you find out something that will spoil the children's chances later. Better to leave it alone and forget all about it." Ralph put his arm around her as he always had when she got wound up, and she let him. Although she was the elder and felt she had to take charge he was taller and was her 'big brother'.

"Look, love, we have found out today that Granddad changed his name so Armstrong will have no meaning in Ormsbury, and I don't look a bit like him so no one will recognise me either. It was all a long time ago, nearly sixty years, so most people might be dead. But I will be careful I promise you."

He could feel her calm down and as she released herself, she said, "I just get that worried about you sometimes. You're still wandering around with no settled job at your age and no wife to keep you on the straight and narrow."

"Look, Sis, I know I seem to have been unsettled and I suppose I have been, this business has preyed on my mind a bit, but the posts I really want are few and far between so if I get this sorted out things might improve. Now then, I've decided not to let the house again but move back here and make this my base. I'm fed up of living out of suitcases."

"But I need my share of the rent, with this credit crunch, Alfie's work has gone down, and with the children growing up things are a bit tight."

"I'll give you what would have been your share of the rent and if my next post is permanent, we'll sell the house and split the money."

"What about the strange woman out there, won't she have something to say about this?"

"Sally's not strange, actually she's quite normal, and she isn't my girlfriend, just a friend who is helping me with the search. She knows more about family history that I do. The house has nothing to do with her."

After a while, the talking stopped and it appeared that the discussion had ended. Ria came back into the front room and found Sally on the stairs.

"You know he hasn't got any money, don't you," she said as a parting shot.

Sally shouted 'Goodbye' after her but was doubtful as to whether she had been heard.

Ralph came back from the kitchen. "I'm sorry you got landed with all that," he said. "I had promised that next time I came over I would go to see her to discuss what to do with the house. I hadn't forgotten I just hadn't got round to it and she saw the car draw up. She only lives up the road. I thought we would have more time before she saw it. But obviously not." He leant against the wall at the bottom of the stairs.

"What's the problem?" Sally asked. "I mean don't tell me if you'd rather not."

"No, it's alright," he replied, "the house was left to both of us by the parents. But because I wasn't married and hadn't got a permanent home of my own, I was to live here as long as I wanted, but if I sold it half of the money was to go to Ria. She wants her money and I can't get a mortgage because I don't have a permanent job. So I let the house and give her half the rent. Now the house is empty she wants to know what is going to happen next. If only I knew too." He lapsed into a reverie for a short while. "Anyway, that's the position at the moment. Unfortunately, she found out about us being at the cemetery. One of the neighbours saw me there and told her. She doesn't like me looking into the past. She thinks that it is best left alone. So that's what all the shouting was about."

"I remember you saying that she did not want you stirring things up."

"Well, now you've seen her you can see what I'm up against."

"I'm glad you put it that way, as I can't say that I've exactly met her. I think she thinks that I'm after your money because she told me you hadn't got any."

"To be honest she has never met any of my girlfriends since I went to university so can't really make any judgements about them so I don't know where she gets these ideas from."

"Anyway, I'm not one of your girlfriends so you're both quite safe. As is the family fortune."

"It's good to know you're not after the twenty pence that is burning a hole in my pocket," he said with a thin smile. "Look this place is OK now. It's quite clean, they have been good tenants, in fact, I'm sorry to see them go. Ria keeps an eye on it so we can leave it for now. Shall we now go and find that meal and decide what to do next? I'm absolutely shattered after today."

Chapter 8

They found a pub which did evening meals on the way to Huddersfield, and over dinner, Sally complimented Ralph on his cleaning technique. "Your mother must have taught you well."

"She always said, leave the rooms as you would wish to find them."

"A good motto. Did she also tell you about girls?"

"No, my Dad warned me about them."

Sally laughed. "He felt you needed warning," she said.

His accent became very broad. "Oh, Aye! Alluss remember lad, there are two kinds of women, them as gives and them as takes. If tha finds one as gives, cling on ta her like grim death 'cos tha'll not find another." Sally laughed again.

"Haven't you found one then?"

"Not until now," Ralph said.

By the time they had finished eating it was getting quite late and as they were walking back to the car Ralph said, "Do you know? I think I'm too tired to drive back tonight. What do you think about finding somewhere to stay the night and go back first thing in the morning?"

"That sounds like a good idea," Sally answered. "The only trouble is, I'm supposed to be in work tomorrow. I only took one day off and I shouldn't take another without organising it first although I could be late. Look, there's no reason why you should come back to Ormsbury unless you want to. Why don't I get the train back and you can take your time."

"Before we decide about that let's find a motel for the night and I can take you into Huddersfield in the morning to catch the Trans-Pennine or whatever it's called these days if that's what we decide to do."

"OK, but I'll have to go early."

Ralph drove on to the M62 to the Hartshead Moor Service area where there is a motel and booked a room. Sally was uncertain about her role in all this but was reassured when he said it had twin beds.

"If I'd wanted more, I would have been a bit more subtle and romantic than a day's cleaning to get my wicked way!!! Besides I'm absolutely wacked and if I'm to get you to Huddersfield in the morning, I'll need my sleep."

That solved that problem. Sally liked him, perhaps even more than just liking but she was a little old fashioned and was not into one-nightstands however attractive the man was. Besides, he was a colleague and embarrassment could ensue after an unfortunate encounter.

It was while he was drifting off to sleep in those moments of drowsiness when reality slips into dreams that Ralph thought "What on earth am I doing? I've dragged this poor woman," and he looked across at Sally drowsing in the other bed, "halfway across the North of England to satisfy a whim." It had been a good day. They had found out a lot, enough at least, to be able to make the search easier going forward and then reaction had set in. His sister, as usual, hadn't helped. Ria had never supported the idea of his quest.

His mind flashed back to the moment when he had decided to look for an answer to the family mystery. It had been around about his thirty-fifth birthday when he had looked at his life and saw that he was really going nowhere. He had his degrees and was enjoying his teaching work but would have liked to do more research but he was not making any progress. He had never achieved tenure in any of the posts he had held and, after his short contracts had ended, he had moved on. Then there was Marsha. They had lived together for, how long was it, almost two years and seemed to be a perfect fit and then she had announced that she was leaving him. For her, his peripatetic lifestyle was no good. She had got tenure and he was on his own. He could still hear her parting words, "You'll never amount to anything!" Perhaps Marsha had been too much like his sister in the end. He had been hurt and had missed her dreadfully, much more than he usually admitted to himself, but he changed jobs and left the area. Marsha had stayed and made quite a name for herself in her field of 17th Century History and Literature.

So at thirty-five, he had decided that this mystery was restricting him. Maybe he was blaming it for his lack of success. He had always been told not to go to Ormsbury. That it was off-limits. So he would go. Not just as a visitor, but to work there, to get to know the people and find out how the place ticked. It had taken him two years but he'd got there. Now here he was in a motel with a strange woman and the mystery was beginning to unravel. It had been a funny old day.

At this point in his reverie, Sally began to snore gently and he fell asleep.

Meanwhile, over in the other bed, Sally too had been considering the events of the day and was looking at her own life. She considered herself to be an independent woman who had made a life for herself which she had filled with as much activity as she could cope with. Those activities reflected her interests and she was, on the whole, happy. Not quite ignoring Pam's teasing about finding her a man she was aware of the lack of a significant other in her life. She wasn't a feminist to the extent that Mary Johnstone was, she enjoyed the male company and she had never ruled out finding a partner, but for some reason the prospects who had suggested themselves had never come to anything. With a wry smile, she remembered the group of students who had plagued her first months at the Brotherton Library at Leeds University. They had been a good crowd, she now realised, and one had been particularly keen on her, but his long lank, greasy hair and his insistence on her going to the Students' Union Bar had quite put her off. She smiled again as she wondered where they all were now. She now realised that she did not even know their names, only nicknames and she had forgotten those. They had gone on to better things as all students must, leaving the permanent staff behind to break in a new batch of students during the next year.

Today had been different; she liked Ralph, although she did not know him very well as yet. Was Pam right and he was the one for her? She had become involved in the personal life of a comparative stranger, and wondering how he would take her involvement, she fell asleep.

The next morning over a very early breakfast, Ralph said, "I'm not coming back just yet. I had time to think last night and I've decided to stay for a while. I need to get my head around what I learnt yesterday and I feel comfortable here. I hadn't realised it until now but this is still home. I've decided to put my furniture back in the house and make it my base for a bit. Maybe the tenants moving out now was just what I needed."

"That's OK. You do what you have to and I'll see you when you come back," Sally replied.

The drive into Huddersfield was almost silent, there did not seem to be much else to say. Ralph waited at the station with Sally until the train came. As they said goodbye, Sally added, "Keep in touch, let me know that you're all right. You've had a shock but it will fall into perspective eventually."

Ralph gave her a kiss on the cheek and waved her off. He had promised nothing.

Once it got to 9.00 am, Sally rang the library on her mobile to tell them she was on her way and would be in as soon as possible. Pam answered the phone and hearing noises in the background asked if she was on a train. Sally said that she was but did not elaborate. The rumour mill would have enough to talk about eventually.

Chapter 9

Sally arrived back at the library at about 10.30 and Pam cornered her as soon as she went through the door. Pam dragged her into the Staffroom where the staff had their breaks unless they went across to the Senior Common Room. Fortunately, there was no one in there.

"Come on, give," she said. "Where've you been, who with and why didn't you tell me before you went? I needed to know in case you needed rescuing," she ended ingeniously. That is always a good reason for knowing everything that is going on.

"Look, if I tell you, you must promise not to tell anyone it is not my secret," Sally replied.

"I promise, cross my heart and hope to die," said Pam.

Sally gave her a brief outline of the family history hunt she was involved with and an even briefer account of what had happened the previous evening.

"You mean, you stayed the night in a motel with Ralph Armstrong, in the same room and nothing but nothing happened?" Pam said when Sally had finished.

"That is precisely what I mean," replied Sally. "Now calm down and put the kettle on and promise again to keep it to yourself."

Pam made a sign as though she was zipping her lips together and said, "Your secret is safe with me." Sally just hoped that this was true.

She did not hear from Ralph for the rest of the vacation. She rang his mobile a couple of times and left text messages but he did not get back to her. She just wanted to know that he was all right. She still felt responsible for his shocked state although as a grown male he was quite capable of looking after himself. Meanwhile, she thought that she ought to find out a little more about a man whom she had found interesting and who she thought was interested in her. Sally, therefore, used her inter-library loan skills to track down and request the two books that he had written. Their titles were rather off-putting and sounded very academic as indeed they proved to be when they arrived. One was on Anglo Saxon poetry and the other on the Norse Sagas. His PhD thesis also proved to be on a weighty subject and was the origin of both books. She found reading them heavy going but at least they had given her an insight into the studious mind of Ralph Armstrong. She did wonder if he was a bit too intellectual for her. However, she took the books home with her to avoid anyone in the library finding them and guessing what she was up to.

Sally did not see him at all until the first Saturday after the Summer Term started when at 11.00 am the doorbell rang and there Ralph was standing on the doorstep with a large bouquet of flowers in one hand and a rather battered attaché case in the other. Sally did not notice when Ralph slid the case behind the settee.

"Where the hell have you been?" was her greeting, "I've been worried sick about you. I left messages but you never got back to me."

"I'm sorry," he said as he pushed the flowers into her face. "I did not pick up my messages until yesterday as I've been very busy. But I'm here now and you can see I'm all right."

She took the flowers and put them in the kitchen. "What happened?"

"After you caught the train, I went back to Cleckheaton and moved my stuff back into the house, which took some time as I had to get it out of storage. The house needed decorating and I got new carpets. I only got back here on Tuesday and lectures started on Wednesday so I've been up to my eyes in it."

Sally put the kettle on. "You're going to think that my answer to everything is to have a cup of tea. But it isn't. I'm only doing this to stop me hitting you with the kettle."

Ralph was about to speak again when she interrupted him to say, "Hang on a minute. Wait 'til I calm down." As she walked past him, he pulled her to him and kissed her. "You know I fancy you, don't you? I've been wanting to do that for a long time, but you never stand still long enough."

"I suspected you enjoyed my company but I sometimes get a bit tongue-tied and never know how to respond. With new people I never feel really comfortable until I get to know them better. So I usually say stupid things. I'm better in a working environment where I know what I'm talking about. That's why I was glad you wanted help looking for your family."

"You're a bit of a clot, aren't you?" he said.

"I suppose so," was her reply.

"That's sad because you care for people, you cared for me and that's important to me. I suddenly realised that after you'd gone. I didn't ring in case I was wrong. I now know I was right. Only someone who really cared would threaten to hit me with a kettle. Look let's sit down and I'll tell you what happened."

When they were finally sitting down with their drinks Ralph explained. "After the train left, I went back to Cleckheaton and on the drive I thought about what had happened and wondered why I was making such a big deal about it. Because you're right. I am who I am. What happened in the past can't really affect me now, my life is so different from theirs. It's just that it seemed so important to know what had happened and why. So I'm glad that I decided to move back into the house, and make it my base, my home, while I sort out where I am going. So as I said, I did. Move in, I mean. That's why I haven't been in touch. I should have been and I'm sorry. That's what the flowers are for. My apologies."

"Right, so you're back in the house, but still lecturing here until next year?"

"Yes."

"Do you still want to find out why your grandparents left here for Cleckheaton, now you know their real name? Or do you want to forget it?

"Will you come out with me tonight and let me make it up to you and apologise properly?" Ralph asked.

"I'd love to come out with you," Sally replied, "I'm sorry I threatened you with the kettle. Oh lord, it wasn't until you didn't get in touch, that I realised how important our meetings had become to me," she added. "This sort of thing doesn't happen to me. Help. What do I do now?"

"Nothing, just enjoy it."

"You know I wouldn't really have hit you with the kettle."

"I know. Shut up, you are talking too much again." He went and sat beside her on the settee and kissed her again.

"Wow," she said. "Can we take things slowly? I'm new to this and I don't want to get hurt."

"Sally, I think you're worth waiting for," was his response. "Now will you let me take you out in public and let the world know that we are an item? Why were you so worried about gossip?"

"Gossip can ruin a relationship before it starts and I did not want the wrong idea going around. Mind you, your visits every Saturday will have given the neighbours something to talk about. But it was work I was most concerned about. You wanted your personal business kept private and this seemed the best way."

"Stop trying to make everyone happy. It can't be done. What about tonight?" Ralph asked.

"What about tonight?"

"Are you free tonight to let me take you out?"

"Yes, I've got nothing on. Thank you that would be lovely."

"Well, get dressed up and we'll go out for dinner. The last one didn't count. Jeans and T-shirts are out. OK."

"I never wear them anyway."

"I'll pick you up about 7.00. Please be ready. I'd better go now before we both do something we might regret later. See you tonight." He kissed her again and left, leaving Sally in a total tizzy.

About half an hour later, while Sally was still coming to terms with this turn of events the phone rang and it was Pam. "Are you going to be in this afternoon?" she asked breathlessly, "I've just heard something you ought to know."

"Can't you tell me over the phone?"

"No. I'd better tell you face to face."

At 1.30 the doorbell rang and Pam was standing on the doorstep. She was very agitated. As she came through the door, she said, "Sally, I've heard the most awful gossip about you and I thought you ought to know. You will tell me the truth, won't you?"

"Of course. If I can," Sally replied.

"Well, I saw Sharon in town this morning, and you know how she is friendly with some of the students, well one of them told her that you and Ralph Armstrong are married."

"You're joking!"

"No. Apparently you were seen outside Bradford Register Office and he was kissing you so the assumption was that you had just got married."

"Trust Sharon to put a spin on it! She's had me married to every available man who comes into the library. She's even worse than you. At least you're discreet and only plague me."

"I know but is it true."

"The short answer is 'No'. I told you when I got back from Huddersfield what had happened and that was the truth."

"But you only gave me a brief outline. Come on. Did he kiss you?"

"Yes he did, but it wasn't outside the Register Office it was the Record Office."

"Were you in Bradford when he kissed you?"

"Yes, but it was to do with what we had just found out about that family history thing. But things have moved on a bit since then."

"What do you mean? Come on, you've got to tell me more."

"It's only just happened, but he's asked me out tonight and we're going out for dinner."

"Wow, tell me more."

"There's not much to tell. He says that he likes me and this is a first date."

"Are you sure you didn't get married?"

"Quite sure."

"Will you tell me what it was all about?"

"No. Because it's not my secret. But if and when I do get married, you'll be the second person to know."

"Why second? Who'll be first?"

"Me you chump."

After that the conversation concerned others and other matters until Pam suddenly remembered her husband did not know where she was and shot off. Sally was going to have something to tell Ralph that evening.

Chapter 10

Ralph came to collect Sally promptly at 7.00, smartly dressed in a suit to complement her decision to wear the black dress she had worn to the Christmas dance. He drove them to Southport and to the Mediterraneo Restaurant which specialized in Italian cooking. A table was booked and ready and waiting for them on their arrival. Over pre-dinner drinks (Ralph stuck to low alcohol Lager) Ralph asked her how much her rail fare from Huddersfield has cost.

"Why do you want to know?" she replied.

"Because I want to repay you the money."

"Why?"

"I abandoned you in Huddersfield," he said, "the least I can do is pay your fare."

"I don't think so."

"Why not?"

"My father always told me to 'Allus have enough cash with you when you go out with a man, lass, so that you can get yourself home if things go wrong', and I did, so I did."

"But it was all my fault."

"Look we can argue about this all night if you want to but, please, let's just leave it and enjoy the evening. I didn't know you were so argumentative."

"I didn't know you could be so stubborn."

"Well, we are finding out about each other then, aren't we?"

When they were seated at their table Sally told him about the rumour.

"Had you heard it?" she asked.

"No, it hasn't reached me yet but I expect it will next week," was the reply.

"I told Pam about us and explained about Bradford but no more."

"I think the best thing to do is follow my old Dad's advice 'When in doubt, say nowt'."

"How many of these sayings had your Dad got?" Sally queried.

"Hundreds," was the reply, "I make them up as I go along. It's amazing what you can get away with if you have northern roots."

"You're a fraud," said Sally.

He held his hands up, "You've found me out," he confessed. "But I only confess to special people."

"Charm and smarm with it," was Sally's comment. "Do I really want to get involved with this man?" she added.

"I hope so," he said. "You asked for honesty in a relationship and by golly you're going to get it."

"Well seeing how you are in an honest mood; I have a philosophical question for you."

"Yes, but I'm not a philosopher."

"I know, but you are a man."

He agreed.

"If lust is sated, can it turn to love?" she continued.

"Wow! Where did that come from? I only studied Anglo-Saxon Language and Literature not the finer points of human relationships."

"But as a man you should have an answer."

"I think that I had better not answer that on the grounds that it might incriminate me."

"Alright. I was going to ask you for dinner tomorrow but I can't. I'm at rehearsals all day for the 'The Mikado' which is on next week, if you haven't seen the posters, I've put up all round the place."

"Yes, I had seen them but didn't realise you had anything to do with it. Are you in it?"

"Yes, only in the chorus. But we have to get our costumes in the morning while the scenery is put up, then we have a technical rehearsal in the afternoon, and a dress rehearsal in the evening and we might not finish until late."

"How many performances are you doing?"

"Six. One a night for the rest of the week. Plus working all day, but no late evening session at the library, thank goodness."

"So it'll be next weekend before I can see you again?"

"I will be at work. If you care to borrow a book or two, I might manage to be somewhere in the neighbourhood."

"Are there tickets still available for the show? I think I might have suddenly developed a passion for G & S."

"Well if you do decide to come, and you get a ticket, don't tell me which night you're coming. Please."

"What about next weekend?"

"If we don't meet before, come for Sunday lunch and we'll have roast beef and Yorkshires. Homemade!!!"

"That's a date."

By the end of the evening they both found that they had enjoyed themselves, the tensions of previous meetings had evaporated and they were comfortable in each other's company. There was still much for each to learn about the other but time would take care of that.

Chapter 11

The next week was hectic for Sally and between work and 'The Mikado' she did not have much time to think and it was not until Wednesday that she found the battered attaché case that Ralph had brought the previous Saturday. He had not mentioned it at all and had put it behind the settee which was where she found it. As soon as she saw it, she knew where it had come from, but, knowing that it did not belong to her, she left it where it was meaning to mention it to Ralph when she saw him at the weekend.

The rumour mill at College had been working overtime and by that same Wednesday it was widely known that Sally Barton had been seen kissing Dr Armstrong outside the Register Office in Bradford. Seven people asked her what Bradford had that their town hadn't. Three female students, first years, kept looking daggers at her every time they came into the library. Sally threatened to hang a sign round her neck maintaining her innocence, but followed Ralph's advice and said, 'nowt'. Having also heard the rumours, Ralph kept well away from the library which meant that they did not meet again until later in the week.

On Friday night, after the performance, Sally came out of the stage door of the Civic Theatre to find Ralph standing holding a single red rose, which he held out to her. She threw her arms round him and gave him a kiss. "You came," she said. "My first stage door visitor. Thank you. Did you enjoy the show?"

"Yes, it was much better than I expected, and you looked great. I've got the car to take you home or do you want to walk?"

"Where's the car – that way – and I live that way. Let's walk, it's such a lovely night. I feel as though I could float home."

"Don't do that, I might not be able to tether you."

"So you are an Anglo-Saxon Specialist. I've never met one of those before." She gazed at him for a few seconds. "No, you are quite human. I've been thinking about it since last Saturday and wondered if it showed."

"You're making fun of me again," he said, "I do lecture on Jane Austen as well."

"Now that's a combination devoutly to be wished," she said.

"Are you drunk?" he asked.

"Not really, I had one drink out of the dressing room bottle before I came out because I was not expecting you. It was red wine and it goes straight to my head. But no, I am slightly aerated because you came to see the show and you brought me a red rose and I think I love you."

"I think I'd rather hear you say that when you are a little less lightheaded. The walk should do you good." There was a pause.

"Jane Austen, eh! I bet all the girls see you as their Mr Darcy, tall, distant and aloof, but I don't. Well you are tall. But you are neither distant nor aloof with me. Is that a compliment? Or is it all part of your seduction technique? I shall have to wait and see. On the other hand my favourite Austen hero is Captain Wentworth in 'Persuasion' who prizes constancy above all things and loves Anne Elliot when all hope has faded. Now there's a hero to die for."

"You are definitely tipsy tonight. Let's get you home."

"Yes, let's go home, but I'm quite sober. I am only drunk on your presence. I've never had a stage-door Johnny before."

"Well drunk or sober you aren't making much sense."

"I thought I was," she replied. "I've just given you the substance of your next lecture on Austen, off the top of my head, in the middle of the night. Some people, mentioning no names, have to work hours in the library to achieve the same results."

By this time they had reached Sally's front door. She quickly found her key and opened the door with no trouble. Whatever was wrong with her, she was not incapable.

Inside, Sally sat down on the settee and Ralph went to look for glasses. He had brought a bottle of dry white wine to celebrate the performance and the evening. Sally took the glass of wine from him toasted his health and took a few sips. "This is very nice, a little fruity but full bodied," she said.

"You have not made much sense this evening. So please be quiet and let me kiss you." Which promptly he did. After a while he got up to go to the bathroom and when he came back, he found that Sally had finished the glass of wine and had fallen asleep on the settee. She was obviously exhausted, and looked so peaceful lying there, so he made her comfortable and went back upstairs for a blanket. He laid the blanket over her, kissed her gently on the forehead and murmured, "Good night, my love, sleep well, I'll see you in the morning." He let himself out quietly and walked back to collect his car.

As he walked, he realised that she was 'his love' that he did indeed love her and it was a whole new experience for him. He'd had girlfriends before; some had lasted several weeks and others had lasted for only one date. Each in turn had gone wrong. The more serious ones had become demanding of his time and his money and he felt that they were using him. One whom he thought was the right one resented the time he spent researching for his PhD and left him for his best friend. They were now married with three children. The one-night dates usually decided in the morning that he could give them nothing that they could not get elsewhere for less effort and ditched him. Marsha had given him hope that there was someone out there for him but even that was not to be. Sally was different. He had brought her into his problems, without her realising the difficulties, and she had not run when the going got tough but had stayed to make sure he was all right before doing what she had to do. Sally was definitely worth holding on to, however long it took. "Was this love?" he asked himself, it certainly wasn't lust. He had tried lust and it had only got him temporary gratification. Here lust came into it but only as part of love. Then he remembered her question at the restaurant "Can lust sated turn to love?" He knew the answer, it didn't, but now he was willing to see if lust unsatiated could turn to love.

The next morning as Ralph made his way to Sally's for their usual Saturday morning rendezvous, he wondered what welcome he would receive. Sally, on the other hand, was feeling very embarrassed as she could not really remember what had happened the night before so when the doorbell rang, she answered it with a degree of apprehension. As Ralph came in, she said, "Sorry about last night. What happened?"

"I was about to ask you the same question," he replied.

"To be honest I don't remember much after leaving the Civic Theatre."

"Do you want the truth or the short version?"

"Go on, tell me the truth."

"You seemed a little high, definitely exhilarated, drunk even, but you kept saying you were sober. You talked about Jane Austen's 'Persuasion' and when we got back here you had a glass of wine and went to sleep."

"Was the wine red or white?"

"White."

"Ah, that explains it. I had a drink after the show, there was a bottle of dry red wine in the dressing room and we all had some. Only a glass but it was strong.

Then white wine on top. I can't take it. I fall asleep if I mix them. I'm OK if I don't have both. What happened then?"

"I put a blanket over you and went home."

She kissed him. "You are really too good to me," she said.

By this time she had put the kettle on and made the drinks. "I found this case behind the settee," she indicated the attaché case. "I presume you brought it; I seem to remember it last weekend."

"Yes, I found it in the loft in Cleckheaton after I moved back in. It must have been there since Mum and Dad's time."

"Have you opened it?"

"I glanced in but it seems to be old newspapers, so I thought you might like to have a look."

"Do you think that they have something to do with your family mystery?"

"That's what I'm afraid of. I'm not sure how far I want to go with this family history hunt."

"Do you want me to look at it, find out all about your family and then tell you the result?"

"Yes."

"I'll do it with you but not for you. You have got to want to find out for yourself. But I will have a look at the suitcase and let you know what is in it."

"Thanks."

"I can't do it just yet. I have the last show tonight, and then the party. Hey, do you want to come to the party? It starts after the show and goes on 'til about midnight. I promise not to mix my drinks. In fact I promise not to drink any alcohol at all so I won't embarrass myself or you."

"I'll let you know later. Does the invitation for lunch tomorrow still stand?"

"Yes, of course. I'm looking forward to it."

"We'll go for a drive after and you can show me the country."

"Definitely no wine then. You know I'm not going to be able to do any research for at least a couple of weeks. I have to make up the time for the people who filled in for me while I've been in the show, and then there are these Staff Association rehearsals for 'Measure for Measure."

"Are you in that as well?"

"Yes. Only a small part. Jim wants me to play an attendant. I don't know the play at all. Are you in it too?"

"Jim's asked me to be a 'gentleman', whatever that means."

"Jim has a habit after wanting a cast of thousands and ends up using three people, so you end up frantically running round in circles. No, I tell a lie it's not as bad as that, but it seems like it. Should be fun."

In the event, Ralph decided not to go to the party after the show, which was probably just as well as it was late starting and as the hall had to be cleared by midnight it only lasted a short while. Sally had found that she was tired and so was glad when it finished early and she could go home.

The next day was fine and sunny and not really roast beef weather but having promised it that is what they had. In the afternoon, they set off for a drive which became the first of many where they explored the countryside together. Although Sally had lived in Ormsbury for six years she had not travelled far and so this was a journey of exploration for both of them.

Chapter 12

It was on the Monday lunchtime following the end of 'The Mikado' and Ralph and Sally's day out in the country when Mary Johnstone cornered Ralph in his office as he was about to eat his sandwiches. She came in quietly, saw that he was alone, and shut the door behind her. This was very unusual as Mary hardly ever went into other people's rooms.

"You do know," she said, "that there is a rumour going around about you and Sally Barton?"

"Yes," Ralph replied, "I do know about it."

"What are you going to do about it?"

"Nothing."

"What?"

"It's only a rumour. If you start denying them people begin to think that there might be some truth in them."

"Well, that's one way of looking at it," Mary continued. "But can I remind you that another person is mentioned in this rumour besides yourself and that she will have to continue working here long after you have gone."

"Your concern is noted." Ralph replied, "But please don't concern yourself with my affairs."

"Is that a polite way to tell me to butt out of your business?"

"Yes."

"Well, as I suggested you go to see Sally in the first place, I feel a bit responsible. We've had temporary lecturers here before who have left a swathe of broken hearts behind them when they have moved on, and I don't want to see Sally become one of their number."

"I have no intention of breaking anyone's heart," he said, "Sally and I have become friends. We know about the rumours and have decided to say nothing to contradict or explain. The reasons are personal to me and Sally understands that."

"Well, as long as you know what you're doing."

"I'm sure Sally would say the same if you asked her. She's helping me with a project, and we are friends. That is all anyone needs to know. If the situation changes it will leak out in its own good time so I would be grateful if you would say nothing."

"I just wanted you to know what was being said, you know what a rumour mill a place like this can be?"

"Thanks for your concern for Sally but everything is fine."

Mary stood and looked at him for a good minute. She was a shrewd judge of character and could see concern and irritation in his face.

"Right," she said, "I've said my piece. I don't normally involve myself in the goings-on in this place, but Sally is a member of the university valued by both staff and students and I would hate to see anything damage that." So saying she left.

Ralph looked at his sandwich and then at the door, and thought, "If this is what's going to happen over a rumour, heaven help me if news of our dinner in Southport gets out. I am going to have to tread carefully otherwise I could have the whole of the university down on me like a ton of bricks. I wish I could go and see Sally and explain but best not. That would only start the rumours again."

Sally knew none of this and was blissfully unaware of the concern expressed in unlikely places. She enjoyed her job but did not think that her contribution was at all important in the scheme of things.

All through the summer term, Ralph came to Sally's house on Saturday mornings for coffee/tea. By mutual consent, they left the vexed question of when to restart the hunt for George Ashcroft Armstrong's history until a later date. A date that was to be decided by Ralph who still had to come to terms with the fact that he wasn't who he had always thought he was. Because his sister had been so adamant that he should not go poking into past history and disturbing any ghosts that might have been lurking there he was unable to talk to her about it and there really wasn't anybody else besides Sally with whom he could discuss it. As a result, the problem grew in his mind until it reached gigantic proportions, and so he put it firmly to one side to be discussed on another day, which of course never came.

Sometimes, he took Sally out to the theatre in Liverpool to either the opera or ballet both of which they both enjoyed but he did not take their relationship further than this. If asked, he probably would have been unable to explain why. He liked her a great deal. He enjoyed her company. In fact, he realised that he loved her but, because of Mary Johnstone's interference, was terrified of making an unwelcome move and which might result in the loss of Sally's friendship and thus lose his access to her skill in being able to research his family history. In fact, throughout this period of their relationship, he realised that he had no idea how she felt about him.

Sally, on the other hand, was deeply puzzled. She liked him. She too enjoyed his company and their joint theatre trips and the meals out. But he never made a move. Their evenings out sometimes ended with a 'Thank you' and a chaste peck on the cheek. On others, just a 'See you on Saturday' when she was left standing on her doorstep. She could not make him out. She knew she valued his friendship and was loath to push things in case it was the wrong thing to do. Over time, she wondered if he was only interested in the help, she could give him and was being kept on ice until he was ready to restart the search. Her knowledge of men who had been seriously interested in her was strictly limited as she had never been the one considered 'fun' who would leap into bed at the slightest hint of interest. In fact, she had gained a reputation of being too independent and this aura had followed her throughout her life. Actually, she just felt she was better than a quick fling and enjoyed people's company and wanted them to appreciate her for who she was rather than as a sex object.

As a result, they both tended to step around each other in a dance of not quite touching but still linked by an invisible thread, a country dance where hands were occasionally linked but each partner went off in a different direction only to meet up again later in the sequence.

Such was the situation when the appointed day for the Orphans' Picnic arrived.

Chapter 13

The exam season came and went, exams and essays were marked. In the library, the end of year checks were undertaken and the annual attempt was made to get all the materials returned by the students who were leaving. The production of 'Measure for Measure', designed to give the local sixth formers some idea of their set text, was performed by its highly educated, but under-rehearsed, cast to great hilarity by everyone. The sixth form seminar for which it was the backbone was a great success and the Summer Vacation beckoned.

On the fourth of July came the day designated as the 'Orphans' Picnic', and it dawned bright and clear. Not a cloud in the sky which gave the promise of a fine, clear settled day. However, rain was threatened for later but when Sally picked Ralph up in her little car at 11.00 am as arranged, they were determined to make the most of the fine weather. He folded his tall, lanky frame into her Fiesta and they set off.

"I'm sorry this car isn't big enough for you but we haven't got far to go," she said.

"No problem. I've squashed into smaller cars than this in my time. We once got me and four others into a mini, but that was when I was at university," he replied.

They arrived at the Beacon and parked. Sally unpacked the boot with the cool box and the hamper and collected the rug from the back seat. Together they made their way to the monument along the path through the scrubby oak bushes that covered the top of the beacon.

"Best keep to the path if you haven't been up here before. But definitely keep clear of the dips. They're dangerous," she told him.

"Why? What are they?" he asked.

"The tops of old mine shafts. They were blocked off by dropping whole trees in leaf down them until they stuck and then they dropped turves and soil on top to level them off. The trees are now rotting and a heavyweight on top can go right to the bottom."

"I hope you are not implying that I am a heavyweight."

"No. But you are carrying the hamper, and that might just tip the balance against you."

"Is it me or the food you're concerned about?"

"Both."

They laid the rug out between the base of the monument and the outlook point, with its pointers indicating what was in which direction, and sat down to look at the view.

To the west, stretched the western plain which led down to the sea and its distant view of the Great Orme at Llandudno. In the distance to the east, the Pennines could be seen beyond the industrial cotton towns of the East Lancashire. Nearer was Winter Hill, standing high over Aglezarke Reservoir, which was the only other hill in the area. From this height, even Parbold Hill seemed small.

"I'm sorry that it isn't Cleckheaton but it's the best we can do around here for some hills," Sally confessed.

"I'm not so bothered about Cleckheaton, but I agree on the need for hills. I am finding this place too flat for my liking."

"I'm the same. I come here all the time to recharge my batteries. But just looking at the Pennines makes me pine for them. The trouble is I sometimes feel like Moses standing on the mountain looking at the Promised Land and knowing that he will never get there when I come up here and look at the promise of Yorkshire."

"It doesn't take long to get there in a car."

"True, but it's finding the time. Besides, it's much more fun to go with someone than on your own."

They unpacked the picnic which consisted of pâté, salad and crisp French bread. There was a bottle of wine for Ralph and elderflower cordial for Sally, as she was driving. They sat and munched companionably while gazing over the view. But then Sally noticed that Ralph was gazing at her instead.

"Now what about this Orphans' Picnic? I thought that there would be more people," said Ralph.

"You didn't really believe that?" said Sally.

"Well, I remember reading about Orphans' picnics in the past when the whole buslofads went out for the day."

"You didn't think that they still had them, did you?"

"Oh, yes, I'm really quite gullible, you know."

"I didn't know. I was under the impressions that you were a highly intelligent and well-educated young man who would not fall for a line like that."

"Ah, but you didn't know how anxious I was to fall for a line like that. 'Orphans' picnic' I ask you."

"And you accuse me of being a nut case. Well, we're here now so best make the best of it."

"Did you really think I would need a hell of a lot of persuading to come out at your invitation?" asked Ralph.

"I have very little idea what you think of me," Sally replied.

"I would have thought after all these weeks, that you would have got some idea of what I think of you. We've been out together, I know we've kept it quiet, but then I rather liked the idea of keeping it a secret. But I think I am falling in love with you."

"That is very flattering and a terrific boost to the ego but I'm not sure that it is a compliment."

"What, that I should find you attractive and fall in love!"

"No, that you should wait so long to declare yourself."

"So you are so used to men declaring themselves on the top of this hill that you take it as a matter of course."

"Can we start this conversation again I think I got lost halfway through."

"Here goes. I hope you realise how much is resting on this. Sally Barton, I think I have fallen in love with you, I would like to marry you…"

"You dear, sweet, old fashioned thing. I thought that marriage proposals went out with the miniskirt. I thought these days it was 'Hey you, get your knickers off and let's see what you're made of', with commitment lasting until the job was done."

"Will you be serious I'm trying to ask you a question."

"Sorry."

"I think I have fallen in love with you," Ralph began again, "I would like to marry you but…"

"I do like the 'but'," said Sally.

"…But I can't ask you to marry me until we have found out about my grandfather." Ralph finished in a rush.

"In that case, we had better hurry up and sort him out," replied Sally.

"Does that mean that if I asked you, you would say yes?"

"I think that it really does," said Sally. "Aren't you rather old fashioned for this day and age? I have been expecting you to try and seduce me into bed before now."

"But you have never given me any encouragement or gave me any hint as to how you feel about me," replied Ralph. "You mean that if I had tried to get you into bed it would have been welcome?" He added after a pause.

"I think I have been falling for you for a long time. But because you never made a move, I decided that I wasn't your type or that you were reluctant to risk losing the chance of finding out about your grandfather if it went wrong" (if only you knew, thought Ralph) "or that you would have found it embarrassing because we are colleagues. However, I certainly enjoy your company and when you go home on Saturday afternoons, I feel low for quite a while. And I look forward to Mondays when you might come into the library and I can see you in the distance."

"That is an amazingly cynical approach to relationships."

"When you've suffered from unrequited love as often as I have you develop a shell as far as men are concerned," Sally explained.

"Well, having got that out of our systems I have got something else to say to you and I don't know how you are going to take it. There is some bad news, and some very bad news and some not so bad news. Which do you want first?"

"Let's start with the bad news and work towards the not-quite-so-bad."

"My contract has only one more year to run but it won't be renewed, Anglo Saxon is being dropped. I have applied for a job in York, but I will be here for another year."

"What does that mean for us?"

"It means we have another year before we have to make any major decisions. Can I ask you a personal question?" he asked. "We have spent a good deal of time together over the last couple of months and yet I still don't know where we are going. I know that I love you and I think that you love me but you haven't actually said so."

Sally frowned. "Actually I did tell you I loved you but I don't think you believed me."

"When was that?"

"The night you walked me home after 'The Mikado'."

"I thought you were drunk if I remember correctly."

"Maybe I needed to be drunk to say it, but you're right. I find it very difficult to actually say 'I love you', but I do, I really do. The last few months have been the happiest of my life, but I am having great difficulty putting it into words. It's as though if I say it, I will lose control of my life, and I suppose I would put my life into your hands and I don't know if you want that responsibility. Can you understand that?"

"Have you ever been in a relationship before?"

"No, I have had boyfriends but none that meant as much to me as you do. It's frightening sometimes."

"Would it make you feel more comfortable if I asked you to marry me?"

"If you did that, then I would know where I was. But don't ask unless you want to."

"Well then, will you marry me?"

"Yes. Oh, yes. Are you quite sure? I haven't just forced you into this have I?"

"No, I've wanted to ask you for a while, but wasn't quite sure how you felt. I want to know that if I get offered the job in York that you would come too."

"Yes, of course, I'll go to York. I love York. I have nothing but my job to keep me here. None of my family is here. I can go anywhere. For a horrible moment, I thought you were going to tell me about a first wife and ten children."

"No. Idiot. I'm being serious. If you carry on like this, I may change my mind."

"No you can't, I can sue you for breach of promise."

"No you can't it's no longer a crime."

"Damn. You did just ask me to marry you, didn't you?"

"Yes."

"Thank goodness, I'm just checking. It's all been a bit of a dream."

"If I get the job in York you will come with me?"

"Yes, of course. Do you know what?"

"Go on."

"I think it's time for this." And she kissed him slowly and gently which lit them both up, and he responded by kissing her passionately in return. After some time they came up for air.

"Do you know," she continued, "I don't have any fears about saying 'I love you.' In fact, I'll say it again 'I love you; I love you; I love you.' Oh, my darling I do love you."

They lay on the rug looking at the sky and began to count the clouds, which was strange because there weren't any.

"Do you think we're mad?" asked Ralph.

"Very possibly," replied Sally, "but only in a nor'-by-nor'-west kind of a way."

"What are we going to tell everyone?" he said.

"I don't know," replied Sally, "but just at the moment I would like to keep it our secret." And then she nearly spoiled the moment by saying, "Just in case the wife and ten children turn up."

"Let's get this straight from the first, I am not married, I have never been married, in fact, you are the first woman I have ever seriously contemplated marrying. Have you got that?" She nodded. "Good so let's hear no more about it. That's how rumours start."

"Sorry. It was only a joke. But I could not believe someone like you had managed to stay single until you are what, thirty…"

"Thirty-seven. Now you know."

"Well, seeing as we are being honest, and you wouldn't dare ask, I'm thirty-five."

"I could ask how it is that someone like you had managed to stay single until thirty-five."

"If I knew the answer to that my life would have been very different. Not better, only different." Sally lapsed into thought for a few moments and then said, "Doesn't the future look rosy? Your job is coming to an end and you could go anywhere but you decide that now is the time to launch into a relationship which could potentially tie you down to one place. But that is not going to happen. I can work anywhere. I am not so wedded to my career that I could not give it up for the man I love. What I would really like to do is research, historical research, and I could do that anywhere as long as there is a library, and I can get a job in a library, any job, not just a career grade job. So it looks as though you have chosen your very own researcher as a companion."

"As you say, doesn't the future look rosy?" at that moment a black cloud which had been lurking in the background began to drop large drops of rain which made Ralph's next suggestion even more relevant. "Do you know what I feel like doing right now?…Let's get back in the car, I'll fold myself in, and let's head for the hills."

"Which hills?"

"There is only one lot of hills we in the north know of. The Pennines. Let's elope to the Pennines."

They hastily packed up the picnic remains and all the paraphernalia as the rain began to fall and ran back to the car, missing out all the dips in the ground, climbed in and set off towards the distant Pennines. The words "We are totally mad" could be heard as the car sped down the road towards the M6.

Chapter 14

As Sally drove along down into Newburgh and on towards Parbold Hill and the M6, she asked, "Can we have a recap?"

"Of what?"

"What has just been decided? You asked me to marry you but you can't marry me until we find out about your grandfather George. Is that correct?"

"Yes."

"So are we engaged to be married at some mythical point in the future?"

"Yes."

"That's all right then. Just checking."

"Are you really happy with that?"

"Yes, it gives me time to get my thoughts together and get used to the idea. I've been on my own for so long that I may find it hard to adjust to being one of a couple."

"There is no hurry. We'll know when the time is right."

As they were driving up Parbold Hill Ralph asked, "How far are we going?"

"Why?"

"It's a bit cramped in here," was the reply.

Sally glanced across to the passenger seat. Ralph was seated as low down in the seat as he could get, but he was so tall that his head still touched the roof of the car, in addition, he had the hamper squashed on his knee as they were in such a hurry to get out of the rain that they did not open the boot to put the picnic in.

"Well, I did think of taking you to the ends of the earth but as you're a bit squashed, we'll stop here," she said and pulled into a parking space at the top of Parbold Hill. From here it was possible to see the whole of the West Lancashire Plain and out toward the sea. In the other direction, Wigan lay and the M6 and the Leeds-Liverpool canal which snaked down to the crossing at Gathurst.

The rain, a shower, had not reached this far and had gone south towards Haydock. Sally got out of the car and went round to the passenger door to relieve

Ralph of the hamper. She opened the boot and put it in, as well as the rug which was on the back seat. Ralph climbed out to help. Then together they stood and looked at the view.

"Will you promise me one thing?" he said.

"Yes," Sally replied warily.

"When we elope, can we go in my car?" Ralph laughed.

"That seems reasonable," Sally replied seriously but with a twinkle in her eye. "But if we are going to elope, I'll have to show you where the ladder is first." She burst out laughing with delight at the whole situation. She put her hand out towards him and he responded by putting his arm around her and drawing her towards him and kissing her on her nose.

"Do you know?" he said. "This is turning out to be one of the better days of my life."

"I sincerely hope it is the best so far," said Sally.

"Would you like ice cream?" he asked and when she nodded agreement, he walked off towards the ice cream van parked in the lay bye. He was gone quite a long time and when she looked for him, he was nowhere to be seen. Then she noticed him walking back across the road from the direction of The Wiggin Tree Restaurant.

"Just sorting out a little surprise for tonight," he said as he handed her the vanilla cone. "I am going to say no more. Now, when we have finished these, will you drive us back to Ormsbury and I will pick you up at 7.00 pm this evening."

Ralph picked up Sally as arranged and drove her to the top of Parbold Hill and into the car park of The Wiggin Tree Restaurant.

"I hope this will be a nice surprise," he said as they walked in.

He had booked a table in the conservatory annexe with a view that took in the whole of the West Lancashire Plain and parts of the Fylde coast to Blackpool. It was still daylight and being midsummer it did not get dark until late but the daylight was beginning to fade to dusk and the sun had dropped down the sky. As the dusk deepened, they could see the lights coming on across the whole area. They twinkled as the evening wore on until finally the sun sank below the horizon far out into the Irish Sea and the dusk grew darker as night fell. It was magical and just suited the mood of both of them. Their table was by the window and on it stood a wine cooler with a bottle of champagne

As they ate, they talked. "It's been quite a day," said Ralph. "I did not intend to propose to you today," he began, "but then it seemed right and so I did."

"You've no regrets then," replied Sally.

"No, none. Why have you?"

"No. But it has all been so sudden that I wouldn't have been surprised if you had."

"My only worry is that I want to get this damn mystery solved before I can feel that I can get on with the rest of my life. How do you feel about that? I mean you could be putting your life on hold while you wait for me."

"There are two things here," Sally replied. "One, do I want to marry you, and the answer to that is 'Yes I do'. Two, will I wait while the mystery is solved and the answer to that is more complicated. The mystery may never be solved. We may never find the answer. So, how far do you want to go with it? Must you find a complete and total answer or will finding out as much as we can be enough?"

"When you put it like that," he said, "it sets it in perspective." He thought for a little while. "Do you know, I think finding out as much as we can, will do. I suddenly had a vision of myself in years to come having let my life, and you, slip away while I tried to find the answer to an unanswerable riddle like a character in a Henry James novel. I always find those characters intensely irritating and feel like shouting at them 'For heaven's sake you've only got one life, live it.' So you're right. Let's find out as much as we can about George and why he ended up in Cleckheaton, and why none of us should come back here to Ormsbury, and let's get married next spring." He finished in a rush.

Sally smiled at him. While he had been talking, she had put her hand on his where it lay on the table and when he finished speaking, she gave it a squeeze. "That sounds like a plan to me," she said.

"Nah then, lass," said Ralph adopting his Yorkshire accent, "is there any one I should see about wedding thee?"

"Nah, tha's not," was the reply. "You are a dear old-fashioned thing, as I seem to have mentioned before. But no, there's only my brother and I'm sure if you asked him, Les'll tell you that he has been trying to get rid of me for years."

"What would your father have said?"

Sally laughed. "Dad would have been alright. Firstly, he would have asked you if you could have supported me in the manner, he would have liked me to become accustomed to, and having made sure of that, he would have shown you where the ladder was kept."

"The ladder?"

"Yes, so we could elope. To save himself the expense of a wedding. He was a Yorkshire man after all." Ralph laughed too at this. He realised that he would have liked Sally's father.

"So what's the plan now?" Sally continued.

"As you know I'm going to Keele to lecture at the summer school at the end of next week and then in August I'm going climbing in the Lake District with the lads from Uni. Which gets me to September, when I go for the interview in York. So I'm afraid I'm going to be busy. As I said, I wasn't planning on getting engaged. However, I will come round this way to see you whenever I can."

"I'm going away in August with Lynne. I've told you about her. We've booked a cottage in Dumfries and Galloway for a week. And then I'm going down to Les's before term starts, possibly about Bank Holiday. Apart from that, it is work."

"If we're still in the Lakes when you come past call in to see us and meet the lads. I've never introduced a girlfriend before it will give them something to talk about."

"And you must meet Lynne. She's my oldest friend."

"Does that mean she gets to say whether or not it's a good idea that we should get married?"

"No, I make up my own mind about things like that. Do you know, I rather think I would like to keep it quiet, just between the two of us for the time being and enjoy the notion that I know something no one else does."

"So no announcement that's OK with you?"

"I'm fine with that. I've no one here that needs to know and I won't tell Ria until we're ready."

"And I won't tell Les either. In the meantime, when I've got a moment to spare shall I start looking into George?"

"Would you mind?"

"No, but I won't spend any money 'til I see you. I know you gave me *carte blanche* with your credit card but I don't like spending other people's money if they aren't there. I'll just sort out what we need to know and see you first."

By this time the sun had set and they had finished their meal and their drinks and realised just how late it actually was. They got up. Most of the other dinners had long gone but the restaurant was not yet closed. They went outside into the velvety darkness and just outside the door Ralph drew her to him and kissed her gently at first then more passionately when she responded. He held her tightly to him as though he was afraid, she might slip away. He was right, she was the one for him. Sally found herself holding him tight as she returned his kisses with an equal passion. She quite surprised herself but enjoyed the experience. 'We're going to be alright,' she thought.

Chapter 15

The next day being Sunday, Sally thought that as they had made no arrangement to meet, that she would not see Ralph again until after he came back from Keele. He was due to go to Cleckheaton to sort his house out before he went and to have his car serviced by his old friend school, Graham, who ran a garage in the town.

She was rather surprised, therefore, when, that evening Ralph came at 7.00 pm and after greeting her with hugs, kisses and flowers they settled down on the settee.

"Now, where were we?" he asked. Sally's reply staggered him.

"We had agreed to a joint venture, which if successful would be mutually beneficial."

"In other words…" Ralph interrupted.

"In other words, you asked me to marry you and I said, yes."

"Why on earth did you put it like that?"

"To give you the opportunity, if you had changed your mind after a night's sleep, to withdraw the motion from the agenda without further discussion."

"Are you totally bonkers?" he asked.

"Probably, but I have never been in this position before and was terrified that it was all a dream. I wasn't sure how you would feel after a night in your own bed."

It came to him then, suddenly, that even after his heartfelt proposal and their dinner last evening, that she was still not sure of his affection and this was her way of trying to find out without appearing to be too clingy. She wasn't one of those women who are constantly requiring and demanding words of affection but she still needed to know. This independence of spirit was what endeared her to him. He had to do more than giving a smile with kind words. Sally looked past those into the heart, and in his case appeared to like what she saw but was aware of the easy way some men could smooth-talk their way into a woman's bed, and Sally wanted more than that. He, in his turn, had to meet her on an equal footing and be as honest with her as she was being with him. He realised that she genuinely wanted him to be honest with her and was, in turn, trying to make it easy for him to walk away if that was what he wanted to do. She wasn't asking him for reassurance and fair words, she really needed to know what he wanted.

"No," he said, "I haven't changed my mind. I couldn't wait to see you; I've been thinking about you since I left and I just could not go to Cleckheaton and Keele without seeing you first."

She took the flowers, which had laid on the dining table, and put them in the kitchen, when she came back, he took her in his arms and gave her a big hug, "I've waited ages for someone like you," he said. "How am I going to exist for the next three weeks, I do not know."

Through the fabric of his jacket, Sally said, "I thought women were the sentimental ones."

"Don't you believe it," said Ralph, "It's just as bad for us. O Lord, this feels good," he added giving her a final squeeze.

"Have you had something to eat?" asked Sally, "I can easily make you something."

"No, I'm OK. I just wanted to see you again before I dashed off on my travels. I'm going first thing in the morning now I've sorted the flat out. Look I must rush off. I'll see you when I get back."

Monday was a strange day for Sally. She had wanted to keep her engagement secret for the time being and that seemed fine but once at work, she found that she was bursting to tell someone. She knew that she could not tell Pam in confidence because it would be around the campus before she could count to one, and so had to sit on it. As term had finished there was plenty to do as tidying the library now became a priority and the stock checks were to be done. As these all took time, she did not have time to ponder on her situation. After the first day, it became easier and by the end of the week, she found that the secrecy suited her. There were no jokes or enquiries from Pam as Ralph, like most of the academic staff, had disappeared for the summer. Only Sally knew where he was. Their secret was safe.

When Sally was not working, she began to look for George Ashcroft. She knew from past experience that family history is a story of fits and starts and the only way was to keep going. After a bit of hunting and pondering, she isolated two birth entries in the births, marriages and deaths who could be him. She also found his death reference as well as his marriage and made notes of them too. She found a possible date for the birth of Ralph's father as his birth certificate had disappeared. But faithful to her promise to Ralph she did not send for any of them. When Ralph returned, she would have something to tell him.

Chapter 16

During the two weeks that he spent in Keele, Ralph began to wonder if the suddenness of his proposal had been the best way of doing things and he wondered if Sally was entirely happy with what was happening. On his return, he called on her and it was while they were drinking their hot drinks that Sally realised something was not quite right.

"What's the matter?" she said. He said nothing. "Are you all right?" she continued, "Not having second thoughts, are you?" Again he said nothing. "You've come down to earth with a bump, haven't you?"

"I don't know," he said, "I feel as though I've been hit by a bus. I've been wondering if we haven't rushed into this and that you might have made a mistake in saying 'Yes'."

"Are you having second thoughts about it? Well best to have them now rather than later," was all Sally said. "I had my second thought before you asked me. I ran several scenarios over beforehand so I knew what I was going to say. I think you act more on instinct and say things on the spur of the moment and regret them later. I learnt long ago not to do that. But if you want to go, go now before more harm is done. I've had a fantastic time which I will remember for the rest of my life but I am not going to hold you to any promises that you regret now." If she had ranted and raved it would have been easy for Ralph to go, knowing that he would be leaving a harridan behind. However, she was calm and controlled and he realised that this was one of the scenarios that she had prepared for, rejection, and had all along taken everything in her stride.

"It's not me that I'm worried about, it's you. You've been so calm about all this that I can't help feeling that at some point you're going to wake up and say 'Whoa, what have I got myself into?'"

"I love you very much," she answered. "Promise me one thing. Don't try to make my mind up for me. I know that this is what I want. If I change my mind, I'll let you know, but please, don't decide what is right for me. It is all right for you to have second thoughts as long as it is not too long before you have third thoughts."

He went into the hall and stood leaning against the wall. Everything had been so good. Their friendship had developed as he had wanted it to with little input from him, and now he had spoiled it, why? He thought about his life how he had done what he wanted, when he wanted, and now he had come to a halt. His parents were gone, and for the first time in years, he had only himself to think of. He enjoyed his career, and, if he could not make a career in a university, he could teach but he wanted more, he wanted stability. He looked at the pictures on the wall. They were of people and places that were important to Sally, her parents, her brother and his family, the house where she was happy as a child, and Whitby harbour with the reconstructed 'Endeavour' sailing in, and he realised he wanted to be there too. He wanted to be someone who was important to Sally. So what was wrong? He realised that he was afraid of the responsibility he was taking on. Your parents are your responsibility all your life, you know that you accept it. But getting married is a voluntary choice, to take on the responsibility of a wife and family without feeling some apprehension would be insane, juvenile even.

Instead of going out through the front door, he returned to the living room to find that Sally was in the kitchen leaning over the sink. She was turned away from him, with her head bowed. He went up to her and gently turned her around. He saw she had been crying, tears were streaming down her face and when he saw that he became choked himself. He held her close to him with his cheek on her hair.

After a little while, he said, "I have been such an idiot. I love you so much. I look forward our times together so much and you make my life so joyful, what on earth was I thinking of, to even contemplate letting you go. I'm sorry. I was suddenly afraid of the responsibility I was taking on. I am an idiot."

Through her tears, Sally replied, "I don't know why you should be afraid, if we do things together, we'll get through, that's what it's all about. I'm the one giving up my independence, men always seem to carry on as normal."

"Not this one," Ralph said.

"Besides, I don't want to rush into anything, anyway." Sally continued as though he had not said anything. "Let's just take our time and get to know each other better. Besides once we start looking properly into the mystery, we may find the answer fairly quickly in which case problem solved. I've made a start. If not, we just carry on. I enjoy your company and as I've waited all this time until you came along a few more months won't kill me. As long as we know where we are going whose business is it but ours."

Chapter 17

The next week passed in a bit of a blur for both of them. Sally went to work on Monday morning as usual and spent the week doing her normal duties, but also had to plan her trip to South West Scotland which would begin the following Saturday. She had been in touch with Lynne her old school friend with whom she had been on holiday for many years. So she set to and managed all the sorting out during the week and in doing so found the battered attaché case behind the settee. She then remembered where it had come from but not having time to look at it before leaving on Saturday, she put it back making a mental note to look at it when she came home again. "What are we going to do with this?" she thought and almost spoke out loud. "Ralph said to leave it for now. We'll have to talk when we get back."

Ralph, because it was the vacation and he was not restricted to a timetable, had gone off back to Cleckheaton to get his climbing gear sorted and checked before the planned holiday with his university friends. They were camping out and so the tent needed checking as well. What with the move back into the house he had not had much chance to get ready.

On the Saturday following Ralph's sudden return from Keele, they both set off North. Sally drove up the M6 to Gretna Green before turning on to the A75 and heading towards Kirkcudbright.

Ralph, leaving from Cleckheaton, had to travel back across the M62 to the M6 before going north to the Kendal junction and heading into the South Lakes.

Ralph rang that evening to say everything had gone smoothly and all the gang had arrived. The weather looked good for the two weeks and he would ring again.

Sally found herself feeling rather low and was glad when Lynne, coming from Sheffield, turned up at the cottage and the holiday could begin. They were old school friends though Lynne had stayed on at school after sixteen and had gone to university and become a teacher. Sally had left at sixteen to work but they had always managed to go on holiday together at least once a year, mostly to a cottage as librarians do not earn as much as teachers. They had not let this disparity stand in the way of their friendship.

Lynne enjoyed a vastly different lifestyle to that of Sally. She was very outgoing with none of Sally's shyness and had had many, many boyfriends living with one or two of them. She enjoyed music, dancing and a city lifestyle which Sally in her less flamboyant way rather envied but knew in her heart was not for her. She did not enjoy dancing, clubbing, and drinking in the same way that Lynne did, but as in a meeting of opposites, they had remained friends through all the ups and downs in each other's lives.

They spent an enjoyable week together visiting those places of interest which attracted them both and found the countryside inviting. Towards the end of the week, Lynne broached the subject that had been intriguing her all week.

They were sitting in the cottage lounge having eaten their evening snack when Lynne looked at Sally and said, "I've known you too long not to know when something's bothering you, come on, out with it."

"You know we promised never to interfere in each other's lives?"

"Yes."

"Well can I tell you something without you getting mad at me for not telling you sooner?"

"Go on."

"You know I've mentioned Ralph Armstrong to you?"

"Almost constantly, but I won't mention that."

"I know I haven't known him very long, but we get on so well together, we share a sense of humour and he makes me laugh, more than that, I make him laugh in a nice way, with me, not at me, we enjoy a joke."

"Yes," Lynne said rather warily.

"We also like the same kind of music, books and films and he eats my cooking, what more could a girl ask for?"

"Go on where is this leading? Don't tell me he's moving in with you?"

"Well, not quite. He's asked me to marry him and I said 'yes'."

"Wow!!! Congratulations. Why do you think there's a problem?"

"I thought you might think that it's all a bit sudden."

"Look, my dear girl, if you get on together as well as you say you do, then I should snap him up as soon as maybe. He's not got a wife and ten children hidden somewhere has he?"

"I don't think so. I did ask him that, and he said not. Do I believe him? You know men better than I do."

"Does he look harassed? Is he paying alimony? Can he afford to take you out without you subbing him? If the answer is 'Yes' then I reckon you can believe him about that."

"So you think it's a good idea?"

"If he makes you happy then go for it," was Lynne's sage response.

"I don't honestly know. He says that I am unlike any girl he's ever met and while I can't really believe that, I must be different. He originally asked me to help him to do some research into a family secret which until now I have not mentioned to anyone. It was while we were looking into that that we were seen in Bradford and a rumour went around WLU that we had got married."

"You didn't tell me that."

"We were seen outside the Record Office in Bradford and he had just given me a kiss, and someone saw us and thought it was the Register Office and the rumour started. Whether it was how I reacted to the gossip or not, I don't know but he told me months ago that he was falling for me long before I fell for him so he wasn't just after a one night stand."

"Have you solved the family mystery for him?"

"No, not yet, but what we did find out knocked him a bit sideways so we are waiting a while before going on. He did produce a suitcase full of old newspapers that we will have to go through eventually but it will have to wait for now."

"Why? Has he moved in with you? Doesn't he have a place of his own?"

"No he hasn't moved in with me but I think that will come up shortly. Should we live together? We're thinking of getting married next spring. Yes, he has a house in Cleckheaton."

"Are you sure, have you been there?"

"Yes, I am sure, and I have been there. He had been renting a flat in Ormsbury. Look, he's only on a temporary contract at WLU and it isn't going to be renewed. They've decided there isn't enough call there for his main subject, Anglo Saxon, and so he is going to be moving on next summer. He has applied for other jobs and there are hopes for one but the interview isn't until September. Once we know where we are with that, we'll know what to do next."

"Just so long as he doesn't take advantage of your generous, good nature."

"If he does, I'll know where to come if I need someone to tell me 'I told you so'. Everything seems so right with him, I trust him and he seems to want me to keep my independence and be a companion, not a slave. At the moment all I can see is the fun of the next few years."

"Right, now I have talked to you like a mother I will say no more."

"Oh, Lynne! You are such a good friend. I know you're only looking out for me." And Sally gave Lynne a hug.

Too soon the end of the week came and it was time to set off home. Sally asked Lynne if she wanted to come with her to meet Ralph and his friends in Ambleside. Lynne's response was that if God had intended her to climb mountains, He would have given her wings so would give it a miss. She didn't fancy a gang of hearty outdoor types. So Lynne set off for home and Sally set off back down the M6 towards the Lake District.

Chapter 18

The drive down to the Lake District was uneventful and by the time Sally reached Ambleside, she was beginning to feel a little apprehensive. Until now she had not met any of Ralph's friends, and they might be a bit overwhelming, not having been to university herself, she sometimes felt that academics might tend to look down on non-university types. This made her shy in a large company and she knew that there were at least eight of them besides Ralph, who had been climbing together. However, she found the hotel that Ralph had booked her into and rang him on his mobile to tell him she had arrived. They had spoken every day but it was now nearly a month since they had last seen each other and Sally wondered what kind of welcome she would get. In the event, she need not have worried. The whole gang poured into the hotel, Ralph swept her into his arms and gave her a big kiss before turning to his friends saying, "Here she is. I told you she was real, and that I hadn't made her up."

"We could not believe that any girl would be mad enough to get engaged or even contemplate marrying him," seemed to be the general opinion of the party. They crowded around each trying to get in first with a kiss of greeting. Ralph was delighted with the reaction of his friends but was only too glad to edge them away from her. She, in turn, was glad to gain a little breathing space. Working in a library can make you a little sensitive to noise, however generous and welcoming it is.

"Wow," was all she managed to say.

"Look, lads, I've not seen my girl for ages, give us a break," said Ralph "We'll meet you at the pub later."

With whistles and jeers, the gang left the hotel, from which they were just about to be ejected by the porter for making so much noise.

Ralph and Sally checked her into the hotel and went up to her room. Inside they looked at each other a little nervously.

"Hello Sally," said Ralph, he was wondering if she regretted getting engaged to him.

"Hello Ralph," said Sally, and she went to him and put her arms around him and kissed him and he knew everything was all right.

Later that evening in the pub the crowd became aerated after the alcohol had been flowing for some time.

While Ralph was at the bar getting another round of drinks. Tom, one of Ralph's friends, who was a little drunk and definitely full of himself, said in a drawl, "So Ralph has got himself a librarian. What do you do all day, dear, stamp books out?"

"Do you know that is the most irritating thing you can say to a librarian," replied Sally. "You," she continued indicating Tom, "have probably got some high-powered degree, which at the moment you make me doubt, but if you have, it was due to a librarian. Who puts the books on the shelf so that you have access to them? Who makes sure the shelves are tidy so that you can go straight to the book? Who answers your questions when you aren't quite sure what you are looking for? Who washes your face and wipes your bottom? That's right a Librarian. You may know an awful lot about a very little, but who needs to know a little about an awful lot? A Librarian! Which is the more balanced member of society, a highly educated ignoramus, or a well-educated librarian? I leave the answer to you." By this time Ralph had come back with a tray from the bar and caught the end of Sally's exposition.

"Well, Tom, now you know why I like her so much, she knows what she's talking about, and lets no one get away with patronising her."

"But don't they just stamp books out?" said Tom trying to regain the initiative.

"Don't be daft. A library is like an iceberg," said Sally rising to the bait, "the stamping out of books is only a small fraction of the work that is done. The rest is making sure that you can get the books you need. In fact, I bet you didn't even know that there is a philosophy of Librarianship. No! Well, there is. It goes 'every book its reader, and every reader his book'. That's what it's all about. Hang on a minute, I remember you. You're Tom Williams, 'terror of the lower fourth', at least that's what we used to call you in the Brotherton."

"How do you know me?" Tom looked apprehensive.

"Didn't Ralph tell you? I started my career in the Brotherton Library at Leeds University at about the time you were all students there. I don't remember him, possibly because he did not cause us any trouble. But you, Oh, I remember you now. Not one of our brightest and best if I remember correctly. Not a First, I always remember the ones I help get Firsts. So this is you today. What are you doing now? Teaching?"

"No actually, I'm a Merchant Banker," he replied, trying to look smooth and sophisticated.

"So you weren't good enough to teach then," was Sally's final cutting remark. Tom looked suitably deflated as Sally demanded, "Where's my drink?"

"Now that we have all calmed down, I've got something to tell you. This will be my last summer of climbing, I shall have better things to do with my time now," Ralph said. Sally looked startled and gestured 'no'. His companions looked staggered.

"What on earth could be more important than climbing and fell-walking?" "It won't be the same if you don't come." "What's happened? Go on tell us?" the comments came thick and fast.

"Sally and I are getting married. I wanted you to meet her before I told you, and I am going to be an upright member of society from now on."

"This is not my idea," Sally said very emphatically. "If you want to continue with these get-togethers it's all right by me."

"I know, love," Ralph continued, "and I know some of you are married and your wives don't object to you coming," "Yes they do," came back in chorus. "But I'm making a commitment and I'm giving it to you straight, so I just don't give an excuse next year and the year after as Harry did and then never come again."

"So this is the last fling of the old gang," said Bill.

"I'm afraid so," replied Ralph.

"I know you organised this year's get together," said Sally, "Why not continue coming but let someone else do the organising?"

"Yes, good idea," was the response of the company.

"No, I've made up my mind. It's time I changed. I'm not twenty-one anymore. I've really enjoyed this summer, possibly because I knew it would be my last with you lot, but it's time to go."

Chapter 19

Sally went back to Ormsbury the next morning. Ralph went back to the campsite quite late, late enough to give his friends something to talk about but only Ralph and Sally knew the truth. So far, their relationship had not been a sexual one but they both knew that when the time was right it would be and from the way they both felt it would not be long now. In many ways, they were rather old fashioned and prepared to take their time. They had all the rest of their lives ahead of them and there was no rush.

Ralph had another week's climbing ahead of him and then it was back to Cleckheaton to put his gear away. Sally was working and the following weekend, being August Bank Holiday would see her heading south to spend it with her brother and his family as previously arranged. Until the rest of the world knew about their plans, they would keep to the arrangements that could not be altered. These were the last few weeks of singledom and secrecy when they could hug their secret to themselves and enjoy each other's company without pressure from outside.

The Bank Holiday weekend passed only too quickly. Sally told her brother, Les, she might be getting married.

"Don't you know?" was his response.

"Well, yes, I do know," was Sally's reply 'but we are keeping it quiet for now as Ralph doesn't want to get married until next Easter. Actually, that's not quite fair. We both decided to wait until Easter, but he has a reason why he wants to wait and I'll go along with that. We haven't announced it yet to avoid undue pressure. He has a job interview next week and when we know the result of that we'll know what we are doing, and when."

"In the meantime, you're keeping it quiet?"

"Yes, no one at work knows yet, but Ralph has told his old friends and I'm telling you."

"Can I tell Mags?" Les asked.

"Yes, do it on the QT when I've gone. I don't want a fuss just yet."

The next week passed quickly enough and the first Saturday in September came and with it Ralph who was driving over from Cleckheaton in time to take Sally on a prearranged trip to Skipton.

At 7.30 in the morning, Sally was leisurely getting up when she heard a car draw up outside. There was nothing unusual in this as parking was allowed on the street, but in the next couple of minutes, she heard a light tap on her window. She ignored it at first but when it came again only louder, she investigated. On opening the window and looking out, she found Ralph standing on the pavement below and about to aim another pebble at the glass. She leant out, being careful to protect her maidenly modesty with her dressing gown, and enquired, "What the devil do you think you're doing?"

"Rapunzel, Rapunzel, let down your hair," was the reply.

"I repeat what are you doing?" Sally said again, but this time with a laugh.

"It's a beautiful morning," Ralph replied, "I know I'm picking you up later, but I couldn't wait so here I am." He flung his arms in the air.

"Why now?" she said.

"Well, I thought, if you had nothing else on, we could elope, and let me take you away from all this. Just tell me where the ladder's kept and we'll be off."

"You're mad."

"I know but only in a Nor' Nor' East sort of a way. Now, where is that dratted ladder?"

"I'm coming down to let you in, or you'll wake the neighbourhood. Some of them like a lie-in on Saturday." She was as good as her word.

"It was such a great morning that I couldn't sleep and wanted to see you so I came round," he said when he was safely in the house. "I came back from Clecky last night and my interview in York is on Tuesday so I thought that as things are looking good today and may not be next week, let's make the most of it." He hugged her to him as he said this.

"Whatever happened to Henry James?" said Sally. "The man who couldn't make a decision without finding out the answer to his mystery first?"

"I don't know who you are talking about. Must be some other fellow. You've not gone and got engaged to someone else while I've been away, have you?"

"No, you idiot. Let me put the kettle on. I've got to finish getting dressed."

He looked at her thoughtfully, "I think it would suit you very well," he finally said.

"What will?"

"The kettle."

"This is getting too mad for worlds. Look you make yourself whatever you want, and I'll go and finish getting dressed. I'll be down in a minute."

When she came downstairs again dressed and ready to go, Ralph said," I went to the supermarket on the way and bought us breakfast, so here it is my lady, pray, be seated here." He led her to the dining table where a full English breakfast was laid out.

"I'll never eat all this," she said.

"Maybe not, but I could eat a horse. It won't go to waste."

"Going back to the Henry James thing, I've been thinking while I've been away. Since I've met you my mystery has faded into the background a bit. I know that we'll get it sorted and that seems to have solved it as far as I'm concerned. If you're up for it, and if not, I'm going to have to work extra hard at it…"

"At what?"

"Getting you into bed."

"At last," said Sally, "the truth will out. I've been waiting for this moment for a very long time. I began to think I was going to have to seduce you!"

"Bring a toothbrush and we'll see how far we get," he said.

"You have something in mind?"

"Neutral ground for a start, and well away from here. Bring a toothbrush, the elopement begins now. 'Ah, ha', he said as he twirled his imaginary moustache, 'tonight my dear you'll be mine.'" The last remark was made in a highly theatrical voice.

"What on earth has got into you?"

"You have, my love," was the reply.

Following that hearty breakfast, Sally grabbed an overnight bag and her toothbrush, and they set off. She had no idea where Ralph planned to go. It was his idea; she was entirely in his hands. As they drove on her mind flashed back to that first trip they had taken together, was it only last Easter when they went to Cleckheaton to look for George Armstrong, but it was only a quick thought. Today was so different.

Chapter 20

Ralph drove out through Parbold towards the M6 and then north until they nearly reached Preston and turned onto the M65 and headed towards Colne. The radio was on in the car and as they drove the sound of Mozart's '*La chi darem*' from Don Giovanni came into the car.

"Ah, ha! A song of seduction," said Ralph. "This is really becoming the theme for the day."

"Do you know it?" said Sally, "Shall we sing it?" Into the car came two new voices singing the parts. Ralph had a mellow baritone voice and while Sally's contralto did not do justice to the aria, she held her own quietly. "That's one of my favourites," she said as it ended. "You are full of surprises today. Do you also play an instrument?"

"I have been known to strum a small guitar," he replied. "I used to play in a band at uni."

"Is there no end to this man's talents!!!"

They passed through Colne and onto the Skipton road.

"Where are we going?" Sally inquired.

"Yorkshire," Ralph replied, and at that moment they crossed over the border.

"We have arrived," he said.

"Do you want to stay the night in Skipton or do you want to go home?" Ralph asked.

"Oh, I thought we might stay the night," said Sally. "I have come prepared. I thought we were eloping even though I didn't show you where the ladder was kept."

At this point, Ralph launched into poetry. "A chieftain to the highlands bound, cried 'Boatman do not tarry'…" Sally interrupted him with, "'and I'll give thee a silver pound to row us o'er the ferry.'" They spent the rest of the journey into Skipton reciting alternate verses of the poem.

Ralph drew into the Car Park off the Market Place and found a space with difficulty. Saturday is market day and the town was heaving with visitors and locals alike. As the morning was well advanced, they went and found a coffee shop and had a welcome refreshing drink. The day was hot and despite the air conditioning in the car it had been stuffy. Plus singing and reciting had dried their throats, well, at least that was their excuse.

Afterwards, they went for a look round the castle. Skipton Castle has been a feature of the Yorkshire Dales since before 1310 when the present castle was begun. Originally belonging to the Clifford family it came into the hands of Richard, Duke of Gloucester following the Battle of Towton in 1461. It was returned to the Clifford's by Henry VII after the battle of Bosworth in 1485. It is the place where school parties are taken, and where parents take their children on a day out. As a result, this was not the first visit of either Ralph or Sally but made a refreshing change for both of them on a first visit together.

As they entered the Great Hall Sally whispered to Ralph, "You know Richard III came here?"

Ralph flicked through the Guidebook. "It doesn't say anything about it here," he said.

"No it wouldn't," replied Sally. "He got it because the current Clifford was involved in the death of the Duke of York following the Battle of Wakefield, and his lands were forfeit after Towton."

"I know," he said, "the bloodiest battle on English soil."

"That's right."

"How do you know all this?" he asked.

"Well, seeing as we are getting along so well, I think it is about time that I confess to a deep dark secret."

Ralph looked at her expectantly wondering what on earth was going to come next.

"I'm a fan of Richard III and belong to a society which is trying to improve his image."

"Well, I gathered from your book collection, that he was an interest but I hadn't reckoned on him being a hobby."

"Do you think that you can live with that?"

"Have you any more dark secrets lurking in your past?" he asked.

"Probably but I can't think of any more at the moment."

"Well, in that case, I think I can live with this one. If you promise not to murder me if I disagree with you?"

"That's OK, as long as we can have a civilised discussion about it."

"You are a nut case, aren't you?" he said. "But a nice one, and mine."

He smiled at her. Her secret was out, and it was not going to make a difference. Sometimes academics can be very scathing about amateurs. Together they continued their tour of the castle and then had lunch in the church tearooms.

They then took a stroll along the canal towpath down towards Bradley and as they went, they held hands and talked about the coming week and the importance of the interview in York on Tuesday. At Bradley, they turned and strolled back to Skipton and the car. By now the day was getting on and Ralph said, "We had better find somewhere to stay."

They pulled out of the Car Park and round the side roads and back into the Market Place and then south down towards Bradley.

As they reached the outskirts of Skipton, they came to the Rendezvous Hotel and Conference Centre. Which they had seen during their walk along the canal towpath. "Shall we try here?" asked Sally.

"Looks OK to me," replied Ralph, and he pulled into the car park.

"We've only got minimum luggage, will they let us stay do you think?"

"We will just have to try our luck. We are both over twenty-one."

The receptionist, whose name was 'Andrew', according to the single word on his badge, was able to give them a room and said lack of luggage was no bar to them staying as they were willing to pay. As Ralph signed the registration card he murmured, "O, I'm the chief of Ulva's Isle and this Lord Ullin's daughter."

The receptionist's response had them both in stitches. "Can we expect Lord Ullin and his men to be following you?" he said.

"I'm not sure he knows where we are," said Ralph. "So I think you are quite safe for the moment."

"Very good, sir." was the response.

Once they were in their room, Ralph held his arms out to Sally who came into them willingly. His lovemaking was tender and gentle while he discovered how she reacted and took his cue from her.

Sometime later, they awoke to find that dusk was falling and that they were both ravenous.

"Let's go and find something to eat," said Ralph.

"What a good idea," said Sally.

They dressed and set off to hunt for some food. They found the Bay Horse pub only a short walk along the road from the hotel. It was by the canal and after an excellent meal of game pie, followed by vanilla ice cream with raspberry ripple sauce, they wandered back to the hotel.

As they entered the door, Andrew, the receptionist beckoned them across to him. He leaned over to whisper in Ralph's ear and said, "I just thought I ought to tell you that Lord Ullin came, but I told him I had never heard of you, and that you were certainly not staying here." He gave them both a wink.

"Andrew," Ralph said, "You are gent and a prince among receptionists, and as mad as we are."

Sally leant over and gave him a kiss. They then wandered off to their room.

Sally woke the next morning to find herself held tightly by her lover, and with a feeling that all was right with the world and that somehow, she had come home.

During the journey home, they were both quite subdued. For Sally, it had been quite a momentous experience, though one she had thoroughly enjoyed. Ralph had flashes of déjà vu which recalled his life with Marsha none of which he had told Sally about as yet. Of one thing he was absolutely sure and that was that he loved Sally and he was not going to do anything which would cause her to have second thoughts about him. He realised that this was putting himself under a great deal of pressure and he knew that he would have to talk to Sally about it if their life together was not going to be stressful. Living together is not easy and requires a good deal of give and take on both sides. From his knowledge of Sally, he felt sure that she was capable of adaptation and he just hoped that he would be able to do the same. As a result of all this thought, he was quite surprised when Sally said, "Do you want to move in with me?"

"Pardon?" Ralph said as he dragged himself from his reverie.

"Do you want to come and live with me? It doesn't really make sense if you are renting a flat in Ormsbury and I have got room. I think I might just be able to squeeze you in if you haven't got too much stuff."

"I know we've had a fantastic time," he replied, "but are you sure you want me cluttering up your life as early as this?"

"O! My darling, you have no idea how much I am looking forward to having you around all the time."

"But what about your own space? From past experience, I know that it's important."

"You have past experience?"

"Yes, I've been wondering how to tell you. I lived with someone for a while but it didn't work out and I don't want this to go the same way. That's another reason I've wanted to take things slowly. I don't want you to make a mistake."

"Do you know, this is the first time in my life I am absolutely certain about what I want. And I want you, as we were last night. I know we can't repeat the first time, I'm not that daft, but being with you has lightened my life."

"Sally, you are special, you know. I'm supposed to be the one to say things like that and you go and do it first."

"I'm sorry, I just say what I think, at least I seem to do where you're concerned."

"Don't apologise, never apologise just be who you are. I can live with that."

"Well, you haven't answered my question. Do you want to move in?"

"I would love to and it would make sense. I can give a month's notice on the flat, that's no problem but only if you're sure. Besides it's my interview on Tuesday can we sort it out after that? Then we might know what we are doing."

"Of course I'm sure. I wouldn't ask you if I wasn't. Besides, I haven't told you today how much I love you or even that I do love you. But I do you know, very much."

"I love you very much too," he paused for a moment and then added, "You are the most important thing in my life. I'll do anything you want me to."

"Careful, that sounds too trusting to me, I might have secret urges to send you bungee jumping or something really dangerous."

"I do go rock climbing, you know, and people have been known to get killed doing it. You can't ask me to do anything I haven't contemplated for myself."

"I don't really want to bump you off yet, maybe later when I've grown tired of you." He could tell she was joking by the chuckle in her voice. It was good to have this close an understanding.

"Well, if I get tired of you, I might just go and do it," he replied with a twinkle.

He drove on.

Chapter 21

Ralph spent Monday night at Sally's house, where she gave him all the moral support, he needed for his trip to York the next day. As he was going through his notes for his presentation, he asked Sally, "How do you really feel about York?"

"This is what you want to do, isn't it?" was the reply.

"Yes, it is my dream job, if I get it."

"Well then, go for it, give it one hundred and twenty per cent. I suspected that it was really important to you but I didn't want to go on about it in case I jinxed it and you lost out through worry."

"But what do you get. I know you said you would be happy to come too when I told you about it, but we haven't talked about it much since. We've referred to it as something in the future. But now it is here. How do you really feel?"

"Look my darling, I've tied myself to you and this is important to you, so, therefore, it is important to me. When you get it, I will be as delighted as you. If heaven forbid, you don't, then we go on to the next one. I'm behind you one hundred and one per cent."

"It will mean giving up your job here and possibly your career as well."

"I enjoy my job, I won't hide that but as far as my career goes, I think I have gone as far as I can or as I want to. Above my grade, it's all admin and I enjoy dealing with the readers and their problems and being out in the library. I'm not one for meetings and policymaking. If the boss comes back and says 'can you find the best most efficient way to do so and so' then I'm quite happy to find the answer but to sit through the boring meeting first, no thanks. So if I can find a job which involves solving other people's problems then I will be quite happy."

"Are you sure?"

"Quite sure, so don't worry about me. If this is what you want, then together we'll make it happen."

"You are wonderful. No one has ever put themselves out like this for me before, at least my parents did but no one else. I love you very much."

"That is good to know, as I wouldn't do it for anyone else," said Sally and then continued, "What form does the interview take?"

"Oh, they'll show us around the university and the department, then we'll have lunch, then we have to put on a presentation, then the interview proper, the offer of the post, and then we can come home."

"What time do you have to be there?"

"Ten o'clock."

"So it's an early start. I'll set the alarm clock. What's your presentation going to be about?"

"I usually do the compare and contrast the Anglo Saxon and Welsh traditions of epic poetry," Ralph replied.

"What about throwing them a curve ball?"

"How do you mean?"

"Why not argue that the last great Anglo-Saxon Document is the Domesday Book."

"How do you argue that?"

"Well, Ladies and Gentlemen, the information in the Domesday Book relates to Anglo Saxon England. The names of the original ordinary people are there, the names of the Anglo-Saxon nobles are there in the sense that they appear as previous holders of the lands and to whom taxes were paid. The north of England was harried between 1066 and 1086 and so the population was vastly reduced and so it is now impossible to accurately assess what the Anglo Saxon and Norse north of England was like. Something like that."

"An interesting thesis, but I'm a literature buff, not a historian."

"Never mind it was only an idea. I'll go and set the alarm now."

The next day Ralph set off early to York. The traffic was heavy on the M62 so he was glad that he had set off early even though he arrived in York with plenty of time to spare.

Meanwhile, Sally went to work with her mobile phone in her handbag ready to check for texts from Ralph at every break. She contented herself by doing her daily stint of shelf tidying, followed by a period after coffee on the information desk. During the coffee break, she checked her messages and found that Ralph had arrived safely in York. At lunchtime, he rang her to say everything was going well and he would soon be doing his presentation although he was the last on the list for this. At tea break in the afternoon, there was no message and she began to get worried. At 5 o'clock she still had not heard from him but when she got home there was a message to say that the interviews were over and he had been offered the job and that he would be setting off home soon.

She was delighted but did not ring him as she hoped he would be travelling so just contained herself in patience until he got home. It was well after seven when he arrived. She never heard his car draw up outside but did hear his key in the lock and ran to see him open the front door. Before she could utter a word of congratulation, he threw his arms around her, swung her around and gave her a big kiss.

"It was all your doing," he said, "and I'm going to give you your reward."

"But first you're going to have a cup of tea," said Sally, "and then you're going to tell me all about it."

She pushed him onto the settee and went into the kitchen. When she came back with the cup of tea, she found him fast asleep on the settee. She put the tea down beside him on the coffee table and sat down opposite and looked at him with a little smile on her face. He looked so peaceful. He slept for about an hour and when he woke up and said, "Where am I? Oh, yes I did get home." Sally made him a fresh cup of tea and sat beside him on the settee.

"Tell me all about it?" she asked.

"All the way to York I was thinking about your suggested presentation, so when I was early, I went into the library to check up on the Domesday Book and thought I'll see how things go. There were six of us for the interview, a couple older than me and the rest either my age or slightly younger. We seemed to get on, we talked about football and the new season, would you believe. ("Yes I would," interjected Sally.) Anyway, they showed us around, it's a great campus with a couple of opportunities for you, there's a main library plus departmental ones, plus the Gisburn, which is now in the university, anyway, we had lunch, which was when I rang you. After that things got intense. The presentations were excruciating. Everyone was talking about things they had already done, nothing about what they hoped to do, so I threw in your curved ball. I talked about Domesday and Anglo Saxon England and the Norman assimilation of Anglo-Saxon culture and thought I had made my point and finished. The panel looked a bit stunned and I thought we had blown it. But at tea one of the Professors asked where I had got the idea from and I said, "My fiancée."

He asked what you did so I said, "You were a librarian and historian, that's true, isn't it?"

He said, that if I was getting ideas like that to hang onto you (which of course I mean to do anyway) and then we went into the interviews proper. That's why I didn't get round to texting you at teatime I was a bit stunned myself. After that, it was plain sailing. As I was last to be interviewed and it was getting late, I didn't ring you again except to say I was on my way."

"Wow," was all Sally could say.

"It appeared that they were looking for someone who would take the work of the department forward and not someone who was content to stand on their laurels and I seemed to be the one. At least I am with you behind me. I mean they had read my thesis so knew what I could do and now knew what I could go on to do. Great eh!"

"Oh, my darling, congratulations. I told you we'd make a great team."

"So you did. What made you think of the Domesday Book? Why that?" Ralph asked.

"It was something you wrote in your thesis," Sally replied.

"My PhD thesis?"

"Yes. Why? Have you written others?"

"I didn't know you had read it."

"That was something else I was going to confess to when I got around to it. I borrowed it through inter-library loan or at least a microfilm of it. I must admit linguistics isn't my best subject so I found it heavy going, but good, I could see that. But at the end of your conclusion, you said something about the end of Anglo-Saxon literature becoming the basis for Medieval Literature and the idea stuck in my head."

Ralph got up and reached for his copy of his thesis which he had hidden well out of the way on the top shelf of the bookcase preparatory to moving in. He opened it at the end and glanced at his conclusion.

"You're right," he said, "I did write that. I'd forgotten. I must be cleverer than I thought."

"You probably are. But remember, I read it more recently than you, and it stuck in my memory because it was about the only bit I actually understood. So the Professor in York, while congratulating you on the acquisition of a clever wife, was actually saying 'read your own work'."

"Your comment must have triggered something in my memory to make me go and check an idea I had thought of all those years ago. You're right, we make a great team."

That evening they sat and discussed the future. Now that York was settled, they knew where they stood and Ralph, now relaxed after his hectic day, agreed that the most economical thing to do would be to give up his flat and move his few items of belongings into Sally's house. He only needed to give a month's notice and, whilst he could do that the following day as long as he paid the rent, he could move into Sally's house at once. He could put his belonging into the back bedroom and take anything surplus to Cleckheaton the next time they went. They eventually decided that while this was what they both would like to happen they would not rush things as they were still very new to the relationship and would take things slowly.

Chapter 22

On the following afternoon, there was the first Academic staff meeting for the New Year. Ralph, of course, was due to attend but Sally, as purely an admin person, was not included and stayed in the library. At 4.30 pm she was astounded to see six of the academic staff members come rushing through the library door. At this time she was timetabled to be at the Information Desk so was sitting opposite the door and saw them rush in. She wondered what on earth could have caused a rush from the staff as they were normally so sedate. Instead of heading for the stairs to the upper floors as she expected they came up to her and offered their best wishes and congratulations on her engagement. She came out from behind the desk to be engulfed in a myriad of hugs and kisses. At this point, she spotted Ralph who had come in behind them.

"I'm sorry," he mouthed at her. She raised her eyebrows. He shrugged his shoulders.

She thanked them all for their good wishes, and thought murderous thoughts of Ralph for all of half a second and then realised the news of their engagement must have got out so was prepared for the next event which was a bouquet of flowers arriving and chaos ensuing in the library.

"I think we had better go into a less public area of the library," she said, as Eileen Hanham came out of her office to find out what was going on. "I think this is a bit disruptive," she said.

"I entirely agree," said Sally. So they all decamped to the workroom. Ralph followed them.

"What on earth happened?" Sally asked Ralph.

"I'll tell you later," he replied, "but I was trying to get to tell you it was out before this happened."

"You'd better go before I get the sack," Sally answered, "but I 'll see you at 5.00."

As Ralph left the workroom Pam and Tracy came bursting in.

"Why didn't you tell us? You sneaky thing!" They exclaimed.

"Oh, girls! It happened in a rush and we said we wouldn't tell anyone to avoid a fuss and now it's out, and there is a fuss," Sally replied.

"Why, when did he ask you?" said Pam.

"At the end of last term."

"And you didn't say anything."

"I've said why."

"When are you getting married?"

"Probably next Easter."

"Well I shall expect an invitation seeing as it was me that said he fancied you and to go for it," said Pam.

"When we finally decide what we're doing, you will certainly get an invitation."

The sight of Eileen lurking in the distance trying to answer a reader's question reminded Sally of what she was supposed to be doing and she went back to the Information Desk. It was going to be a hectic few days.

On the way home, Ralph told her what had happened.

"Just as I was going into the meeting one of the idiots in Social Sciences said, 'Hey Armstrong, you jammy devil, I hear you've moved in with Sally Barton.' I couldn't let that pass. The rumour mill could be working overtime in next to no time flat so I thought I'd better put them straight, so at the end of the meeting, we were asked if anyone had anything to say I stood up. I made a speech. 'Colleagues,' I said, 'I should like to inform you that Sally Barton of the library and myself got engaged over the summer and, as I have not yet moved into her house, there is no need for any gossip,' and then I said, 'I count myself a very lucky man, and any of you who were slow off the mark, Yah Boo Shucks to you.'"

"You didn't say that did you," said Sally appalled.

"No not the last bit, but I thought it. I wasn't going to have salacious gossip about my girl. I just wanted to set the record straight as reputations are involved."

"I can see I have found a battler," said Sally.

"You'd better believe it, baby," he replied.

"I love it when you talk Anglo Saxon," laughed Sally.

When they got home Sally went into the kitchen to start preparing the evening meal. Ralph came in behind her and put his arms around her waist and began kissing the back of her neck. Although her hands were wet, she turned within the circle of his arms and putting her hands behind his neck, she kissed him.

"Do you want to eat now or later," she said.

"Later, definitely later," he replied.

"You go and find somewhere comfortable, while I dry my hands and I'll join you," Sally said.

Ralph left the kitchen and a moment later when Sally went to find him, she found him on the settee in the living room.

"Here?" she said.

"Why not?" he replied. So she joined him on the settee.

Sometime later as they were both in a drowsy state Sally asked, "We've never discussed it, but do you want to have a family?"

"Yes," he replied sleepily, "but not until I have found out why I shouldn't have come to live here in the first place. I don't want any of my children to live with a mystery hanging over their heads as I have had to do."

"It is that big a deal for you?" said Sally waking up a bit.

"Yes. Do you know something?" he was waking too, "If you have nothing planned for the weekend, I think we should go to Cleckheaton."

"No, I've got nothing planned that can't wait for another day, we'll go to Cleckheaton."

Sally got up and put on a few clothes and carried on making dinner, while Ralph went to find their bathrobes which they wore while they ate their meal.

"Do you realise," Ralph said, "that if I had not ignored my father's warning and not come here, I wouldn't have found you. I think that I can now face whatever the future holds if I've got you on my side."

They smiled at each other across the table and they both realised that several hurdles had been crossed that day and that they were now working together for their future.

"You are really the most surprising person," Ralph said.

"How do you mean?" Sally asked.

"Well, when I first met you, I thought here is a girl who is calm and controlled and will take no nonsense from anyone, in fact, I found you a little intimidating. But now I have got to know you better, much better, I find you are full of fun, not controlled at all, and full of nonsense in fact I sometimes think I'm going to have to run twice as fast as normal to keep up with you."

"Well, in that case, I shall have to slow down. How about doing everything in slow motion?"

"Now you're just getting cheeky. To think at one time, I thought you might be no fun at all!"

"Shame, I was just getting used to the idea of slow motion. Maybe you're no fun."

Chapter 23

On Saturday Ralph drove them over to Cleckheaton. On the way, they talked of this and that but it was not until they actually arrived outside the door of Ralph's house that Sally began to realise the true significance of what she was doing. Ralph's house was Ralph's parent's house, it was not hers. But at that moment she realised that now, being engaged to Ralph, it could be hers also. Ralph opened the door and said, "I should by rights carry you over the threshold but I'm not sure my back could stand the strain."

"That is not very flattering, besides we're not married yet," replied Sally, "but do you know I don't think I want to go inside yet."

"Why what's the matter?" he asked concern entering his voice.

"I've just realised that his house is part of you, and it's going to be part of me, and I'm not sure I'm ready for this."

"Don't be silly."

"I expect I am being silly, but can we talk about this first?"

"Yes, of course. Do you want to sit in the car?"

"No, let's go for a walk." The set off up the road, Ralph holding Sally's hand.

"Come on, tell Uncle Ralph what the problem is," he asked.

"This is stupid. I really do enjoy being with you, and living with you, but so far, we have been living in my house with my belongings and you've moved in among them. Now I realise that the reverse is true. You have a home and I've got to move into it with you. I suppose I feel that I won't be in charge here. And the responsibility is huge."

By this time they had come to a little park with benches and so they sat down.

"You're not having second thoughts about us are you," Ralph asked.

"Oh no," said Sally, "It's just that I feel out of my depth. Can I make a home in someone else's house?"

"I should think you could make a home anywhere," he said loyally.

"Yes but it takes hard work."

"Stop worrying, it will be all right."

"Ralph, can I ask you a serious question but it will probably sound odd?"

"Yes, go ahead."

"Do you see marriage as a dictatorship, a monarchy or an equal partnership?"

"How do you mean?"

"Well, are you the boss, am I the boss, or do we discuss things and come to a mutually agreed decision?"

"Where on earth did that come from?"

"We have never discussed money. I wondered how you saw us. At the moment I am paying the bills in Ormsbury, and I presume you are paying the bills here…"

"Oh, I'm so glad you've brought that up. I was beginning to wonder how to broach the subject. Yes, I'm paying the bills here, but as I'm living in Ormsbury I should be paying them there as well. I don't consider myself to be the boss. Of your three alternatives, I think I see marriage as an equal partnership."

"Why should you be paying all the bills? Surely we should be sharing them if it's an equal partnership."

"Until now, wherever I hung my hat was home, at least that was my philosophy. I've moved about so much that this is, was, the only home I had until I met you. Now wherever you are is home, I know that now. Mentally I've moved out of here. At least I had when I came a few weeks ago, it wasn't my home anymore, it's just a house where my parents lived. This house is my responsibility. So what about we share the expenses in Ormsbury?"

"I don't think that it's fair that you should pay all the expenses here. Look, let's set up an account for the bills with you putting half in and me putting in the other half, and what about making it enough to cover the expenses here as well, so that they are both ours. When you start in York next summer, we can have a house, a home, of our own where we start from scratch."

"That sounds like a good idea. You earn less than me, will you be able to enjoy yourself on what is left after putting in your share?"

"I don't know until we've worked out the figures but if you think we could make that work then let's do it." Ralph nodded in agreement. "Do you feel better about things now?" he said.

"Much better. Now, what was that about carrying me over a threshold?"

"Do you know, I think I'll leave that until we have our own home to move into?"

They walked back to the house and went in through the front door. Ralph had straightened it and put the furniture back but it had a curiously impersonal feel, as though someone had dressed a stage set. Sally realised it was because there was no personality. It had all the furniture belonging to Mr and Mrs Armstrong, but they themselves were no longer there. Ralph had removed all the personal items when he let the house and while he had replaced many of them when he took back the house, some were now in Ormsbury (as she now realised) and it was just a furnished house.

"Where do you sleep when you've been over to stay?" Sally asked.

"Usually in my old room," Ralph replied.

"Where are we going to sleep tonight?" she asked.

"In my parents' room," was the answer.

"How would they feel about that? How do you feel about that?"

"I don't think they'd mind, we are almost married and they are no longer here, as I said it's just a house. Actually, we've come here because I had an idea."

"Always a dangerous thing to do," said Sally.

"I agree but listen to this one first. I wondered if you would consider living here after I start in York next year."

"You mean rather than looking for a house of our own?"

"No, only if we couldn't find one. I could commute from here if necessary until we could get sorted out."

Sally looked at the house. Yes, it *was* small. Actually, it was slightly smaller than her home but after Ralph put the suggestion to her, she realised that it was a possibility but where would all their belongings go.

"I think we could make it work," she said, "but possibly only for a short time. We have so much stuff we wouldn't get it all in here, you know."

"I realise that having seen how squashed we will be in Ormsbury, but you think it's possible."

"Oh, yes."

Ralph put his arms around her and kissed her. "That is a load off my mind," he said.

"You've been crossing bridges before you come to them, haven't you?" Sally asked.

"I suppose I have," he replied.

"Well, if we are doing things together, I don't think there is anything we cannot overcome."

"I think you're wonderful," he said.
"No, I'm not," Sally replied, "just practical."

Chapter 24

When they arrived back at home in Ormsbury, Sally went into the kitchen and put the kettle on, while Ralph put the bags in the hall. She came back into the living room as Ralph entered. She looked at him. "Hold me," she said.

He put his arms around her and held her close, gently but firmly. She put her head on his shoulder and her arms around him under his jacket so he could feel her warmth through his shirt. He rested his cheek on the top of her head. They did not speak, but so many ideas and memories rushed through their minds.

He thought of Sally. How she had responded to his lovemaking in a generous and loving way; how his previous girlfriends had taken him for granted; how one had insisted on eating an apple throughout his efforts to give her pleasure; how the one he had loved had never made him feel as Sally did; how he had never taken any of them back to Cleckheaton to meet his parents and how he wished they had met Sally. As he held her, a great warmth flowed through him followed by a feeling of tenderness towards her and he suddenly knew the meaning of the word 'cleave' and wished he could promise to 'cleave only unto her'. He knew her, he felt he could say anything to her and she would take it in her stride. He could tease her and she would laugh and not get annoyed. She would never tell him he was stupid because of something that he had said, and she would never take him for granted and he would never take her for granted. He loved her. It was as simple as that.

Sally, meanwhile, was thinking about all the new things that had come into her life in such a rush. One minute she was an independent woman making her own way in the world and the next she had committed herself to a stranger who made her feel that anything was possible; that the moon and stars were within reach; whose lovemaking had shown her worlds she never knew existed; whose ideas she could catch and run with; in whom she could put her trust and know that he would not let her down. She thought of her family and how she had finally come home to this stranger. For the first time, she knew the meaning of the phrase 'the other half'. He was the other half of her. Together they made a whole. Was this what marriage could be? Could it be a deep spiritual meeting of two different people who combined to make one whole person? She was a little afraid that if she let him go, she would topple over because he was providing the balance that made them stand together as a whole.

In the kitchen, the kettle had long since boiled and turned itself off. In the living room, they still held each other.

Sally stirred and without releasing her hold of Ralph she looked into his face.

"Hello," she murmured.

"Hello," he murmured in reply.

They kissed a long, gentle kiss, lacking in passion but full of love. It seemed to last forever.

"Have you been to the same place I've been?" she asked.

"Into the depths of my soul?" he answered.

"Yes," she replied. "Is this what love is?"

"All I know is that with you I have come home," he said.

"And all I know is that you are the other half of me," she answered.

They both knew that the future was theirs.

"I think we ought to have a drink before we become dehydrated and start having hallucinations," Sally said.

"Too late," replied Ralph. "I'm already having them."

Sally's practical streak was coming to the fore, "I'll make you a cup of tea. But first, you'll have to let me go."

"I can't do that," he said, "the dream might fade and I'll wake up. If this is a hallucination, I want it to last."

"This isn't. This is true. It's actually happening, we can't wake up. We've just got to live with it."

"You will insist on having the last word," he murmured.

"I don't mean to," she replied. "Let's have a drink, a toast in tea to the rest of our lives." He released her from his embrace and she went into the kitchen and switched the kettle back on, he followed her and as she stood by the counter, he put his arms around her again.

"I'm not letting you go," he said.

"I don't want to be let go," she replied, "I'm afraid you've got me forever."

"That's all right then," he answered, but continued to hold her while she poured the boiling water into the mugs.

"You'll have to let me take these through to the living room," she said, and he released her.

"I didn't know I could love someone as much as this," Ralph said, "I've never felt this way about anyone before."

"I've never wanted to be as close to anyone as I am to you," Sally replied, "I know that I will love you forever."

"Life is going to be fun," he said.

In the weeks following this spiritual awakening, their lovemaking took on different characteristics. The urgency of the early weeks was gradually transformed into a mutual giving and receiving of pleasure. Sometimes they soared so high that they reached the moon and could touch the stars, at others they lay in each other's arms content in the closeness. Afterwards, Ralph did not turn from Sally and fall asleep, but turned towards her and held her in his arms until they both slept. When it was not possible Ralph held Sally gently putting a large, warm hand on her stomach to ease the cramps of her monthly inconvenience.

Now that this important aspect of their lives had been resolved only the daytime routine needed to be sorted in order to give their lives contentment.

Chapter 25

Before Ralph had come into her life, Sally's routine had been simple. She had had only herself to plan for and work around and to fill her solitary evenings, she had worked late on Monday's until 9.00 pm, and on Tuesdays, she had gone to rehearsals for the Operatic Society, on Wednesday once a month, was the Family History Society meeting and on other evenings were committee meetings and the search for entertainment at the cinema, theatre or concert hall.

Ralph had often spent his spare time in the gym keeping up his fitness levels for his athletic endeavours, or in the pub with colleagues, maintaining his street cred. Sometimes, when he pursued an idea for a project, he would spend an evening in the library of whichever institution he happened to be working. He had never actually stayed in one place for more than two or three years and therefore had a vast knowledge of higher education organisational structure but little permanent knowledge of living in one place. The one constant had been his parents' home in Cleckheaton which he had always been able to retreat to when unemployment loomed.

Now the situation was different. Though they were now living together, they had each other to take into consideration when planning their hectic schedules. As a result, they sat down one evening in the week following their return from Cleckheaton to outline a *modus vivendi* for the coming term.

Here the compromise was to be reached. Ralph readily saw the necessity for Sally working late on Monday evenings and, he resolved to either go to the gym or work in the library until closing time on Mondays. They would have had lunch together before Sally went into work and Ralph would bring her home at nine o'clock. The Family History Society was essential to Ralph's quest and could therefore not be given up. Sally had used her free Monday mornings to do any work needed to support the Family History Society Library and she said that she would continue to do this until the next AGM, the following May.

The other nights were open to negotiation. Sally was prepared to give up the Operatic Society as she would be leaving Ormsbury the following summer when they moved to York, although she would like to give a farewell performance. Sally asked Ralph if he would like to join the Operatic Society as their next production was 'Oliver' but he declined. He felt that one singer in the family was one too many but would not stand in the way if Sally wanted to continue. Although rehearsals had already started, she felt that she would rather spend time with Ralph and so would give up 'the Operatic'.

After having this rather involved conversation Ralph said, "You know, one of the things I really liked was when I came round to see you on Saturday mornings to discuss the search for my background. Not that we discussed it much, but that was why I came. Do you think we could carry on doing the research on Saturday mornings?"

"Ah, ah!" said Sally, "We haven't been together for two months and already you're trying to recapture the excitement of our early relationship. Why not! I managed to find the time before we were together so it should still be possible. So Saturday mornings are for research and the rest of the time is ours. Hurray, I rather like the sound of that."

They began on the Saturday before the term started, when Ralph finally reached for the battered attaché case that had stayed half-hidden behind the settee since he had brought it back from Cleckheaton after Easter. Over the months it had been noticed from time to time by various visitors and commented upon, but it had remained firmly shut and unexamined ever since.

He lifted it gingerly onto the living room table and with Sally standing by released the clasps and opened it. Although he had quickly glanced at the contents of the case when he first found it, he was initially disappointed by the contents. Inside were a number of newspapers. Together they lifted them out onto the table and in the middle of them, they found a silver-framed photograph of a man and a woman.

They looked at the dates on the papers and they all dated from 1951 and 1952. Ralph took the photo out of its frame and looked at the back. On it was written in pencil 'Beattie and George 28 September 1929'. Who were they? Ralph did not know.

Sally looked at the newspapers. First, she put them into date order and found that they were copies of the Liverpool Echo and covered dates in May 1951 and June 1952. The earliest, in May 1951, had a frontpage story which was an account of the murder of a policeman on the Dock Road in Bootle. Each subsequent issue contained further details resulting in the arrest of a Michael Kinsella and this brought the coverage to an end. The papers dating from June 1952 contained reports of the trial of Michael and Barry Kinsella. There was, however, no mention of any Ashcroft in the reports.

"Do you know what?" asked Sally, "I think that we must start again. If we put all the information we have in order, discover what we haven't got and go looking for it. When we have found it, if we do, then we can go forward."

"That sounds like a good idea," replied Ralph, "apart from remembering that my name is really Ashcroft, I've forgotten what we know."

"I know," said Sally, "its ages since we did any family history and from past experience, you forget all the nuances and just remember the basic facts. Besides these newspapers must be important otherwise they wouldn't have been kept so we'll put them back in the suitcase and keep them until we know more. OK."

"Sounds fine to me," replied Ralph. Sally replaced the newspapers in the case and put it back behind the settee. It's amazing what a good filing place that can be.

So they went back to the beginning and found that they did not know very much. All they had done was find George Ashcroft Armstrong's grave and the date he died and that was it. They knew nothing about why he had left Ormsbury and why the family were not to return.

Sally took out her file of notes which she had started months before and looked at it.

"We never got hold of your Grandfather's death certificate, did we?" said Sally.

"Is it important?" asked Ralph, "we know when he died."

"I suppose in the scheme of things it isn't because we have the information, but there can be more details on death cert than the date of death."

"Such as?"

"Cause of death, sometimes, date of birth, and of course where they were living."

"But I remember where my grandmother was living, I remember going there."

"Yes, but she could have moved after George's death and besides its all information."

"You mean information will make us free."

"Something like that," said Sally.

Sally opened her laptop and went online. She looked in the *free bmds* website for 1962 and found the death of a George Ashcroft in the Bradford area in the September 1962 quarter. Having got the reference number she went into the Identity and Passport Service where the General Register Office website is to be found and ordered the certificate. With any luck, it should be with them in about a week. She then went back to *free bmds* to look for a marriage certificate for George and Elizabeth, but as they did not have Elizabeth's surname, they could not cross-reference it. However, Ralph knew the date of his father, John's, birth so could use that as a starting point. They found birth of a John Ashcroft in the June quarter for 1950 in the Ormsbury registration district. They sent for that certificate as well. If they obtained John Ashcroft's birth certificate it would have the names of both his parents on it, including his mother's maiden name which would help them find Ralph's grandparents' marriage certificate. Actually, as you can never guarantee who your father is without a DNA test nowadays, this is now a bit useless. It was originally wanted for inheritance purposes. They looked for a marriage of a George Ashcroft during 1949 and found one in Ormsbury which they thought could be the right one and sent for that as well As the certificates were going to take time to arrive there was not much more that could be done at that stage.

Chapter 26

The following week saw the start of term proper and they began on their prearranged plan of organising their days. Naturally, it did not work out as planned, as these things have a tendency so to do, but it worked well, and with a little tweaking could settle down into a comfortable routine.

By Friday evening the certificates they had ordered, so hopefully, the previous Saturday had not come and so they spent a quiet evening, Sally watching television, with the sound turned off and the subtitles on, while Ralph read a book in preparation for the next week. She had her head on his lap and he had his arm laid across her. They were very comfortable.

At about 10.00 pm Sally said, "It's late, let's go to bed."

Ralph's reply astounded her, "No."

She was startled, "Why not?" she asked.

"I'm not going to come up yet."

"What's wrong?"

"I've got the awful feeling that this mystery is worse than we think. What if George suffered from something so awful that could be passed on, and it made him do something that made it impossible for him to return."

"I think you're getting yourself depressed over this. I don't think George did anything awful."

"Why not?"

"For a start, we would be hearing about it. I've lived here long enough to have heard all the gruesome gossip. There have been a couple of murders that everyone talks about, but there has never been any mention of a George Ashcroft."

"But that could only mean that no one knew what he had done."

"But in that case why leave? And why never come back?"

"You have a point," he brightened up. "He left because of something that happened that he was involved in and people knew."

"Yes. I'm beginning to think that too," Sally said.

"But what if what happened was caused by something genetic."

"You mean he was a werewolf or something in his genes that might come out in your children?"

"Yes."

"I doubt it."

"Why not?"

"Because he lived a perfectly normal life in Cleckheaton until he died, didn't he? Your father never said that he was in an Institution of any kind, did he? Both your father and your mother were perfectly normal, weren't they? And so are you."

"Thank you for that," said Ralph.

"Or at least you are by normal criteria." Ralph laughed. "I'm not afraid of you," she continued, "or for you, and while something might skip a generation could it skip three? Do you think that it could be something to do with the male chromosome? Although I don't think being a psychopath or a sociopath is inherited through the Y chromosome."

"So you don't think I should be worrying?"

"No, that's why I suggested going to bed, we can just sleep, you know."

"But what about you? I know you want children but do you want this as a threat hanging over them?"

"No threat," she said. Sally got up and went into the kitchen and came back with half a glass of water. She gave it to him.

"Is this glass half full or half empty?" she asked.

"Is this a trick question?" he replied.

"No. Whatever you answer, it will tell us about you."

"Well, I think that it's half empty."

"I think it is half full. I think you are a pessimist so you see the negative side of things, whereas I, an optimistic pessimist. Now drink some of the water." He did so. She took the glass from him and drank the rest. "Even though you saw the glass as being half empty there was still enough left in it for you to slake your thirst?"

"In other words, there is a positive side to being a pessimist."

"Something like that. I'm terrible for crossing bridges before I come to them. I have so many alternative plans in case something goes wrong, that I am pleasantly surprised when everything goes right. You are even worse. You think that you will have an accident and get killed before you reach the bridge so, therefore, make no alternative arrangements and get stuck. Let's see how far we can get before we write George off. We've only just started. Besides if we have girls the Y chromosome will disappear and the curse of the Armstrong's with it."

"How come you know so much?"

"Trust me, I'm a Librarian." She laughed. "I don't really know, you know. I make most of it up, like you and your father's wise sayings. But you do pick up a lot of useless and useful information in my job."

Ralph looked at the clock, and he was definitely looking happier now. "I think I might be ready for bed myself now," he said.

Later Sally murmured in his ear. "I forgot to mention that we might never find out why your grandfather left here."

"Oh, I'm so glad you didn't tell me that sooner otherwise we would have missed the last half hour and that would have been a tragedy."

She thumped him gently in the ribs and held him close as they fell asleep.

Chapter 27

The certificates finally came on the Tuesday of the second week of waiting and while the birth certificate told them what they wanted to know, the death certificate did not. It gave the wife, who had registered the death, as Gladys with no second name of Elizabeth which could have tied her to the George Ashcroft they were looking for. So they needed to look for another George Ashcroft. They had found two in the relevant quarter of the register and had obviously sent for the wrong one. The marriage certificate was also the wrong one and the wife's name was Joan Forshaw. However, now they had John Ashcroft's birth certificate they had the information to start looking for George and Betty's marriage as they now knew her maiden name was Elizabeth Grimshaw.

After some minutes checking through possible marriages, she said, "I think I've found it. The trouble is they didn't get married in Ormsbury they went to Preston. I mean they could get to Preston on the train but why go there. It looks as though they eloped." She looked at Ralph. "There's a possibility that eloping runs in your family."

"We'll start with that and see how far we get," Sally continued, entering the information into her computer. "Now if we send for that other death certificate, we might find that we are getting somewhere."

"The only trouble is, we'll have to wait for the certificates to come," she added, "another week to wait. I'm sorry about this, my love, I'm afraid family history is a slow process."

"I'm beginning to realise that."

"Anyway, we do know a little more about George."

"Do you know, I think I've got some old photographs that were taken when I was a child, they're in one of the boxes upstairs? I'll go and have a look for them."

Sally heard him banging about upstairs and realised that it was time to get dinner which she set about doing. Meanwhile, overhead Ralph was having memories which were rather different from the ones he had set out to look for. Among a bundle of photographs taken while he was at Leeds University, he found one of a group of his friends standing on the steps of the Parkinson Building looking very pleased with themselves. Among the group was one girl who looked rather startled and on looking more closely he realised that it was Sally.

Downstairs the pans were nicely boiling when Sally heard a shout from above her head.

"Sally, come here."

"What do you want? I'm busy." was her shouted reply.

"Sally please come up here." Reluctantly she came up, after turning all the pans off, he had after all used the magic word. "What do you want?"

"Look at this photograph. Do you recognise anybody in it?"

Sally joined him sitting on the floor and took the photograph and looked at it closely. She could see it was of a group of young people all laughing and joking on the steps of the Parkinson Building, but as she looked and tried to put names to the faces there was one girl she recognised. Then she remembered, it was when she was a library assistant in the Brotherton a gang of students had dragged her outside to have her photograph taken.

"I recognise the steps," she said. "There's you," she said pointing, "and Tom Williams, the 'terror of the Lower Fourth' he was at the camp in Ambleside, and one or two of the others, Bill somebody, and Kenneth. That's me, but I don't know the other girls."

"Don't you remember? We had just got the results of our finals and we were celebrating and taking photographs so we wouldn't forget the feeling or the day and we kidnapped you out of the Brotherton to remember you as well."

"I remember now, it was my first end of the year. I'd gone to work there in January and I was overwhelmed by it all. There was this student, with long greasy hair which fell over his face, who kept asking me to go to the Student's Union Bar for a drink and I wouldn't go. Mind you I don't think I ever saw his face properly and I think he had spots. He used to mumble when he asked me and I used to have to ask him to repeat what he'd said. I'd been to a folk night or something in the union Bar with one of my colleagues and it was full of noise, smoke, and boozy students, not my kind of place at all. I don't think I'd recognise him again."

"You didn't. I mean you haven't. Do you mean if I'd asked you to go to the pub you'd have gone?"

"It was you," Sally was suddenly overcome, "but, but you had long greasy hair, and you haven't in the photograph."

"I'd had it cut that morning; it was my lucky charm. I'd decided that if I let my hair grow and didn't wash it my brains could not possibly leak out and I would get a first."

"And did you?"

"Yes. Hence the exuberance. I've never done anything so daft since."

"I remember you now. If only you'd cut your hair sooner and suggested the pub, who knows what might have happened. On the other hand, you never asked me out looking like that and you never came back to see me, so it was probably only a student crush."

"It was. I hadn't thought about it in years 'til I saw this and recognised you and remembered. I fancied you something rotten then. I used to lurk around the issue desk trying to work out a strategy to get you to come out with me."

"You wouldn't have liked me then. I was young for my age, and still finding my feet in the big world. You were all so sophisticated, at least I thought so. I didn't trust you. Besides one of my colleagues had said to only go out with students when you think you can handle them. And I couldn't, not then. I had a lot of growing up to do."

"I think that was part of your charm. I thought it would be easy to get you to come out with me because you were young and I tried all that summer, but you had the strength of character that I did not expect and in the end, I gave up. The rest of the gang called you 'the one that got away'. They teased me about it for years. Your strength of character is still there, I've done the growing up."

"If this is what you have been waiting for all these years, then you had better have it now," and she kissed him as only she knew how. "We won't tell your mates about it. Let them work it out for themselves."

Sally left him to get on with what she had been doing and he continued looking through the packets of photographs and ruminating on then and now. Then he remembered he had done some more lurking in a library watching a girl and he realised it was the same girl though nearly eighteen years apart. Then, he remembered they had called her 'Sarah Brown' after the prim and proper heroine of 'Guys and Dolls'. What was it about her that had attracted him so? Then, he had thought she would be an easy conquest and was astounded when his youthful good looks and boyish charm had failed, mind you, he thought, his chat up lines had been pretty feeble. Now, when he had had the world at his feet and any number of girls had fallen at them, to come back to the same girl when both had changed out of recognition and to find that love was there, that was something to be wondered at.

Later over dinner, he said, "I remember you at the Brotherton now. We called you 'Sarah Brown' from Guys and Dolls. The Students' Union Drama Club had just put it on."

"I remember," replied Sally, "I went to see it. But didn't Sky Masterson ask her out for a bet?"

Ralph began to look uncomfortable. "You didn't have a bet on me going out with you, did you?" asked Sally, "You did, I can tell by the colour of your face."

"I'd forgotten that," said Ralph looking sheepish.

"Well, I suppose you can collect your winnings now. How much was it for?"

"Five pounds, which was a lot in those days. Anyway, I can't collect. You had to have come out with me by results coming out."

"So that was why I never saw you again. If only you had persisted, with short hair who knows?"

"Now you're teasing me," he said.

Chapter 28

They waited expectantly until the following week brought forth the expected certificates. In the meantime on Wednesday Sally asked at the Family History Meeting if anyone had any information about a George Ashcroft who had disappeared in the early 1950s but had had no response.

When the certificates finally arrived late the following week the envelope was waiting just inside the front door as they came home from the university together. Ralph opened the envelope. The first certificate they looked at was George's death certificate. It told them that it was Elizabeth who had notified the registrar and that George had died in a motor accident while driving a trolley bus in Bradford and his address was given as 32 Field Street, Cleckheaton.

"Field Street," ruminated Ralph, "that was where grandma lived. That's where I remember going to see her. There was a big field at the end of the street and I used to go and play on it when we visited. Ria was too grown up to play with me so I went on my own. So she didn't move away from there. She must have felt safe and settled there with my dad even after all those years on her own."

"Shall we go and have a look at it next time we go over?" asked Sally, "I expect it will have changed a bit since then."

"No. I don't think I want to. I went up there several years ago and it has changed. The street is still there but there's a housing estate on the field, I think I'd just like to remember it as it was," replied Ralph.

The other certificate was exciting. "*The marriage certificate of George Ashcroft, aged 21, and Elizabeth Grimshaw, aged 21, at Preston Register Office on 20 December 1949.*" it read. The fathers' names were given as George Ashcroft and William Grimshaw. The interesting thing was that both had given their ages as being 21, and Sally and Ralph knew from George's gravestone that he had been 32 when he died in 1962, which meant that he had been born in 1930 and was only 19 when he got married

"This cannot be right," said Ralph, after he had looked at it long and hard.

Sally took it from him. She looked at it in thought. "Why did they get married in Preston?" she then asked. "If they had parents' permission, they could have got married in Ormsbury, no problem. And why does it say they were of 21. If you work back from their ages on the gravestone George could only have been 19 at most and Elizabeth 18. They must have lied about their ages; they didn't have parental permission and they got married in Preston. I'm sure by then you had to produce proof of age when getting married, so how did they get round that?" She continued to think. "Damn," she said. Ralph looked startled; Sally did not normally swear. "I forgot the National Service. George should have been doing National Service unless he was exempt for some reason. Also, look at the date. They got married five months before John was born. There was a certain urgency about it."

"I don't know what you think?" said Ralph. "But I'm finding all this a bit complicated. I know you've had more experience of doing this sort of thing than I have, once it gets to later than 1400, I'm lost. Perhaps you could explain all these expletives to me."

"Let me think about it first," was the reply. Sally reached for a pencil and some paper and began to make notes and draw a rough family tree. Eventually, she seemed satisfied with what she had written down.

She showed the paper to Ralph and said, "As far as it goes so far this is it. Your father was born on 30 May 1950 as John Ashcroft. His parents, George and Elizabeth, were married on 20 December 1949. George's father was another George Ashcroft. What was puzzling me was that George and Elizabeth got married in Preston and gave their ages as being over 21. But, on George's gravestone and on his death certificate, it says that he was 32 when he died in 1962 which means that he was born in about 1930, so therefore he was only about 19 when he got married. Also, there was National Service at that time and he should have been in one of the armed services unless he had been exempted for some reason. It was often educational, you did it after leaving university, if you didn't have some illness, like rheumatic fever, which affected your subsequent health. So why wasn't George in the Forces? Why did he lie about his age? What was going on?"

"You mean that there's a mystery inside a mystery?"

"It looks like it. I mean if he had heart problems would he really have got a job driving a trolley bus in Bradford. Wouldn't he have been too big a risk? I'm going to look for George's birth certificate next and see how far that takes us.

We haven't got enough information to fill in the gaps or answer those questions at the moment."

"Look, you're doing a great job tracking all this down, don't get downhearted. Just find out what you can, even if we never find the answer, at least we tried."

"Bless you, my son, now I think we'd better have something to eat before we fade away. It's been a long week. How do you feel about going over to Cleckheaton tomorrow and put some flowers on the graves? Then, if you like, we could go on to Leeds and I'll show you where I was brought up."

"That sounds like a great idea, let's get out and about. I think I'll go to the gym for a workout to clear my head can we eat later?"

"No problem, we'll eat about eight. While you're out, I'll have a look and see if I can find a birth certificate for granddad George. We've got quite a lot of information now so I should be able to find some George Ashcrofts in the right year." So while Ralph went out to blow the cobwebs away in the Gym, she started checking births on her computer. She came up with three possible and made a note of the references. In the end, she sent for all three in the hope that one was right. She felt that they were getting very close to the end of the search and was not going to waste any more days waiting for the wrong certificates.

Chapter 29

The following day they had their day out in Leeds and after calling in at the cemetery in Cleckheaton they set off for Ormsbury. On the journey, Sally said that she was feeling as though she was getting flu. When she arrived home she went straight to bed after assuring Ralph that she would probably feel fine in the morning. However the following morning she felt no better and asked him to tell the library when he went into WLU, which he did. She stayed in bed all that day but felt no better in the evening so on Tuesday he rang and asked for a visit from the doctor. As he had no lecture until the afternoon, he stayed with her until the doctor arrived.

"I think I know what it is," the doctor said, "but I think you had better go to the hospital for some blood tests." So Ralph bundled her up and she staggered downstairs as she was feeling very weak and he drove her to the hospital, where, after what seemed like a considerable wait, the blood samples were taken. The results would be sent to her own doctor so they immediately rang to make an appointment. The next day they rang the doctor again to find that Sally had developed a glandular fever. She would be off work for at least a month as the effect of the disease is to cause weakness and lethargy. There is no cure and she just needed to rest and take plenty of fluids.

The doctor came to see them. After explaining about the disease she asked Ralph who was going to look after Sally.

"It's me," said Ralph. "Her only family live down South and can't come here they have their own lives. Plus they have young children. We're engaged and I can move in to look after her. Will she need a great deal of attention?"

"No, not really," was the reply, "She needs plenty of fluids and rest but while she may be quite weak at times unless something goes very wrong, she should be all right."

Sally kept apologising, saying, "You did not know what you were letting yourself in for when you got involved with me. I'm afraid this is not going to be very fair on you."

"Don't be daft," Ralph replied, "I was planning to promise to take you for better or worse up to now it's been better, now we're just having a bit of the worse sooner than we expected. I'm not sure what to do but I'll look after you as best as I can."

"If what the doctor says is true, and I am just weak, if I can look after myself, there shouldn't be any nursing I'll just need food and watering. So if you could do the shopping and a bit of cooking, we'll manage."

For the next month, they took things very quietly. Some days Sally felt stronger than others and was able to read or watch television. On others she slept and ate very little, she lost weight but managed to keep up with her fluid intake and after about three weeks she began to feel stronger.

"The worst thing is," she said to Ralph one morning, "that I can lie here in bed and think of all the things I could do when I get up because I feel so well, and then when I get out of bed I am so unsteady on my feet I think I'm going to fall over and it takes me all my time to climb back into bed. It is so frustrating."

"Never mind," he responded, "I can see that you are much better than you were two weeks ago. You are eating more and getting about in the house, though I can't see you going back to work soon. Not until you are eating properly, you won't have the strength."

"You mean I'm going to have more time off?"

"Yes. I'll ring for the doctor to come and see you again and we'll see what she says."

"Can you find me a quiet, non-active job to do for you? I'm beginning to get bored."

"Why don't you have another look at my family problem, something might have gelled while you've been ill."

"What a good idea. If my mind is working properly, I could do that, and when it goes to mush, I can watch TV."

"I'd better go," said Ralph, "you come down when you're ready I'll leave the breakfast out for you."

It took some time for Sally to get herself out of bed and into the bathroom and down the stairs. She had not dressed, in fact, she had not got properly dressed for weeks and she was beginning to feel very lazy and neglectful of herself. Ralph said nothing about this but she knew that as soon as she started being stronger that was the first thing she must do. He had been so caring, helping her have baths and making sure she was eating that the least she could do was to do as much as possible for herself. She had been ill for almost four weeks and while actually having a diagnosis helped her come to terms with what was wrong it didn't help her get better any quicker. "Therefore, today," she decided, "I will start to make an effort." She came downstairs just as Ralph was leaving for WLU.

"I'm going to make an effort today," she said as he kissed her goodbye, "I'll get dressed later and have dinner with you at lunchtime."

"Don't promise too much," he said. "I'll ring the Doc and let you know what happens."

About an hour later the phone rang and it was Ralph. "The Doc says that you should be up and about by now so won't come to see you, can you go to see them. I've told them about the situation and you can go this afternoon at 2.20 pm. How do you feel about that?"

"I'm OK at the moment. I'll be there I'll get a taxi."

"OK. I'll see you just after 12.00," and he rang off.

She was really going to have to pull herself together even though she still felt weak.

Sally knew that whatever their plans had been for living together the glandular fever had altered them. Ralph had moved in. He had set himself up in the spare room so as to be on hand if she needed anything. They now shared a room but if she was tired, he slept in the spare room. Having sat down she looked around her. There was a stack of unopened post on the dining table which she thought was mostly junk mail but when she looked closely at it, she saw that letters were mixed up with it. It was all addressed to her. Ralph had obviously opened his own and not troubled her with hers.

She reached for the letter opener and slit open the envelopes. There were 'Get Well' cards from friends and three certificates from the Identity and Passport Service. She put these on one side and put the cards on the mantelpiece. There was also an envelope from her Richard III society with the latest issue of the magazine. In it was an article she had written herself. She carefully put it on one side so that Ralph would not see it. Unfortunately, it became mislaid and she did not have the energy to hunt for it.

She was getting better. Sitting down on the settee she reached for her 'George Ashcroft' file and sorted the certificates into it. Ralph had thoughtfully put a bottle of water by the settee and she was about to reach for it when she thought "No, I'll have a hot chocolate for a change."

She got up and cautiously walked into the kitchen. There was already water in the kettle so she switched it on while she reached for a mug and the chocolate. By the time the kettle boiled she was ready. However, the full mug was too heavy for her to hold in one hand so she stood in the kitchen leaning against the cupboards while she drank it. What an achievement! When she finished, she left the mug in the sink and made her way back into the living room.

Sitting on the settee she again looked at the 'GA' file as she called it and put the certificates that they had accumulated in order. The certificates that she had just opened gave the parents as Joan and Harry, Mary and John and George and Beatrice. Which of them were the parents of Granddad George? There could only be one. George's marriage certificate had said his father was also George and there was only one George on these new certificates. She, therefore, ignored the ones with Harry and John and concentrated on the one whose parents were George and Beatrice.

That made her think. George and Beatrice, otherwise Beattie. She looked around for the attaché case and located it beside her desk (it had a habit of moving). She managed to reach the desk and opened the case and took out the photograph. 'Yes. It did say George and Beattie on the back'. They must be GA's parents. Progress. She was still sitting at the desk when Ralph came home.

"How are you feeling now?" he said.

"Much better," she replied. "I decided this morning that you had looked after me long enough and I must do more for myself. To be honest, I don't feel strong enough to go back to work yet, but I'm getting there. I haven't done much this morning but I have found this." She showed him the certificate and the photograph.

"So, these are my great-grandparents," he said.

"It looks like it," she responded.

"I wonder what happened to them?" he mused.

"We'll sort that out later," Sally said. "First lunch, then a taxi, then the Docs, then solve the mystery."

"That's right get your priorities in order. The great Librarian's mind at work," he teased.

"I bet you are so glad that I'm so weak, otherwise you'd pay for that," she returned, as Ralph went into the kitchen to make sandwiches.

Chapter 30

In the event, Ralph went to the doctor's with Sally as it was Wednesday and he had no lectures or contact time scheduled for that afternoon. The Doctor was very pleased with Sally's progress but said that she needed more time to recuperate and was not to go back to work for at least another two weeks. They left the surgery feeling relieved that Sally was improving but sorry that it was taking so long. As Sally climbed back into the car she said, "Darling, I'm so sorry you've had to put up with all this. I'm sure you didn't think that when you found me the first major hurdle was to look after a sick woman. I wouldn't blame you if you asked for your money back."

"How do you mean?"

"Faulty goods, under the Trade Descriptions Act."

"You really are a nut case, aren't you? I wouldn't change you for the world. Besides, I'm finding things out about myself I didn't know."

"Such as?"

"Well, I can now cook proper food, under your guidance of course, and ironing. Wow! Who knows where that might lead? Could be the odd bit of dusting?"

"I thought your mother taught you all that."

"She did, but I lied, I'd never actually done it on a regular basis."

"I think I'd better have a look at the Trade Descriptions Act. Perhaps, after all, we're both frauds and have been found out."

"At least we haven't been found wanting. We've coped, haven't we?"

"As usual you're absolutely right. I do hate you. In the nicest possible way of course."

By this time, they had arrived home and Ralph helped Sally out of the car but she was able to walk into the house on her own. As she had not been outside for the last three weeks this was a big improvement. However, she was very tired and lay down on the settee to rest and soon fell asleep. Ralph meanwhile sorted his lecture notes out and did some reading of 'Northanger Abbey' for his next set of lectures on Jane Austen. When he had exhausted Austen, he got out his trusty copy of Beowulf and passed an hour overcoming Grendel. When he was lost in Anglo Saxon England all the troubles of the modern world disappeared for a while and he came back to them refreshed.

When Sally awoke after about an hour and a half, she found Ralph on the settee beside her, also asleep. She looked at him in wonder. He constantly surprised her. The love and care that he had showered on her over the past few weeks had overwhelmed her. She had thought that most men would run away at the hint of a problem but not Ralph, he had faced it with her. She felt so lucky to have found him. After a while, he stirred and woke.

"Oh! You're awake. Do you want a drink?"

"That's a great idea. Shall I make them?"

She struggled off the settee but refused to let him help her. "I must do this for myself," she said. She went into the kitchen and put the kettle on, filling it via the spout using a mug as a measure. She did not trust herself to lift the kettle when it was full of water. She got down two mugs and reached for the tea bags and in doing so knocked one of the mugs onto the floor. "Damn and blast," she yelled and thumped the working surface as hard as she could with the palm of her right hand. "Ow," she cried and burst into tears.

"What's happened?" asked Ralph coming into the kitchen.

"I've broken a mug and hurt my hand, and I can't do anything right," sobbed Sally. "I'm so ruddy weak it's frustrating."

"Come and sit down, let me do it."

"I wanted to start doing things myself."

"You will as you get stronger. Look why don't you think about making dinner tomorrow night then you'll have all day to get it done and we'll both enjoy it tomorrow. Let me do things today."

She leant against him. Her tears were beginning to dry. It had only been a momentary lapse.

"That sounds good to me. I do so want to get better."

"I know you do." He took her back into the living room and sat her on the settee and he went back into the kitchen and made the drinks. He brought her hot chocolate and put it beside her on the coffee table.

"I've put plenty of milk in it so it won't be too hot."

"Right," she said. "Today has not happened. We start today tomorrow and I will be better."

Chapter 31

Over the next two weeks, Sally began to get out and about. She went for short walks, always making sure that she had somewhere to stop and lean against if she got tired. Her appetite was returning and she was eating better and she felt stronger. She was pottering more in the house and she actually was stronger. In the last week, she took out the attaché case again and looked at the newspapers.

It was then she realised that the last one had an account of a car accident in which a couple had been killed. The headline, 'Local couple in a motor accident' had not given much information but her eye caught the name Ashcroft and she read further. George and Beattie Ashcroft had been killed by a hit and run driver as they waited for a bus in Maghull. Was this their George and Beattie? She would have to go to the Public Library to find out more. This gave her the motivation to go out and find out.

The next day Sally felt strong enough to walk to the Public Library she took a pad of paper and a pencil and set off. She made it with only one stop for a breather and asked for the back issues of the local paper which were, as she had suspected, on microfilm. The librarian kindly threaded the machine with the film for 1952 and she soon found June. She looked carefully through each issue until she came to the one which covered the date of the Liverpool Echo which was safely stowed in the attaché case at home. She looked at the next issue and page by page she checked to see if there was any further information. There was an account of the accident, however, the driver of the car which had killed George and Beattie had not stopped. The make and model of the speeding car had been identified and it was hoped that the perpetrator would soon be caught. Sally next looked at the Deaths column and there was what she was looking for. Under Ashcroft, it read: '*George and Beatrice 24 May 1952. The tragic deaths of George and Beatrice Ashcroft are announced. The dearly beloved parents and Grandparents of George, John, Sheila and Jean and baby John, they will be fondly remembered by all their relatives. The funeral details will be announced later after an inquest has been held. Any enquiries to Wortley & Co, Wigan Road, Ormsbury.'* Sally called the librarian over to her.

"Is it possible to get a photocopy of this page?" she asked. The librarian showed her how to do it. Fortunately, Sally had taken some money with her and as a result of this request, she was able to copy all of the pages that she wanted. She continued to look through the paper and finally found that the bodies had been released for burial about a month later and that the inquest returned a verdict of 'death by manslaughter against a person or persons unknown'. The police had been unable to trace the car involved. Sally made copies of all the relevant articles and with her booty returned home.

When Ralph came home that evening, she was able to tell him about all she had found out.

"Do you remember the photograph that was among the papers you brought from Clecky?" she said. "Well, I think it is definitely of your great-grandparents. Your grandfather's birth certificate was amongst the post that you put on one side while I was ill and it said his parents were George and Beatrice or Beattie. Today I went to the Public Library and found out about the accident. Do you remember those old newspapers? One had an account of an accident on the front page. I looked at it again this morning and found that it related to a George and Beattie Ashcroft so I went to the library to look it up and this is what I found out." She handed him the pile of photocopying that she had accumulated and he read through it.

When he reached the end, he looked at the photograph and said, "I think you're right. These are the same people. But why have we got the photograph now?"

"I don't know. I haven't thought as far as that. I was just trying to get facts. But as they died suddenly perhaps George wanted something to remember them by. The trouble is that while we know that he came from here, and left never to return, and didn't want your father or anyone else coming back, we don't know precisely when he left. If he had the photograph and these newspapers it probably means that it was after the accident but how long after, and why, we don't know."

"Is this as far as we can go?"

"There's just one last chance," Sally answered. "The death notice in the paper lists other children. They may be still alive, and in the area. If we can track them down, they might be able to tell us more."

"You mean I've got relatives I know nothing about? Of course, you do. I've been living in isolation with this for so long I hadn't thought about other relatives. There were only just us."

"We have got names now from the notice. We can start by looking for Brother John as he will be an Ashcroft. The sisters could have married and will be harder to trace. Do you know, I think we are getting somewhere at last!"

Chapter 32

On 21 November Ralph arrived home with a large bunch of long-stemmed red roses.

"These are for you," he said giving them to Sally.

"What are these for?" she asked.

"To celebrate our anniversary."

"Which anniversary?"

"The anniversary of the day you said you might have to kill me. It's exactly one year since you refused to tell me the secret of the classification system."

"Have I just discovered your secret?" Sally stated. "Ralph Armstrong, you're an old romantic."

"I didn't know it was a secret. I've never made it one, but I suppose, yes, I am a romantic at heart." was his reply.

"How come?" she asked.

"I started with dungeons and dragons. When Graham and I were about 10 we set off to look for one. We thought that there must be at least one dragon somewhere nearby. We could see Emley Moor so thought that it might live there. So one day we set off, with a wooden sword and some sandwiches. We'd told our mothers we were going fishing. Of course, we never got there. It was miles away. Do you know there is a severe shortage of dragons in Cleckheaton?"

"Get away. I don't believe you, there must be at least one."

"No not one. However, when I was about 13, I discovered girls and spent quite a time trying to find out what made them tick. I still haven't found out. Then for A levels, I was introduced to Medieval Literature and the poems and songs of courtly love, Sir Gawain and the Green Knight, and Mallory's King Arthur. I mean there had once been such things as dragons and girls who needed rescuing. Actually, I just think they wanted to get laid by a hero. But that's my theory. So to university and the discovery of Anglo-Saxon Literature, and I found modern girls just wanted to get laid by anybody so heroes were out of fashion."

"So what did you see in me?"

"You were the first girl who threatened to kill me if she told me a secret or a mystery. I suddenly, for an instant, saw it as something out of John Buchan. You know, when Scudder tells Richard Hannay that the secret, he is about to tell him might get him killed. I knew that you had a romantic soul too. I knew that you were practical but romantic too! That was more than anyone could hope for. Then you took me to the top of a mountain."

"Come off it. Ashurst Beacon hardly counts as a mountain."

"It does to a romantic. So I proposed. Then you suggested eloping. How romantic was that? I mean did you only want to get laid? But I was willing to take the chance."

"What made you think I was a romantic too?"

"Look at your books, you noodle. Your interest in castles, Richard III, Charles I, even King John, all 'wrong but romantic'. Of course, you're a romantic. Serious with it though. I mean, you don't let the romance get in the way of the truth, but you like the romance too."

"You have been working all this out, haven't you?" Sally said admiringly.

"It takes one to know one," he replied.

"I've got another idea. I've been thinking," said Sally.

"Always a dangerous thing to do," replied Ralph.

"Well, I've been pondering, then."

"On what, or should that be 'what on'?"

"You should know, you're the literature expert in this family. Anyway, whatever. I've been thinking that we are the sum total of our life experiences up to now."

"How do you work that one out?"

"Well, we met at Leeds University, didn't we? Right. I didn't take to you at the time, or the situation was not right or our stars were in the wrong place or something but we didn't get together. Since then, you've gone to Oxbridge, and I stayed on at Leeds and did my courses and qualified as a Librarian and came here. You got your PhD and became an expert, and came here, where we met again, but didn't recognise each other from all those years before. We are now different people. We have had experiences which made us who we are now. This time when we met, we gelled, perhaps the time was right or our stars were in the right place but here we are. So far it is working. So the people we have become are perhaps the people we should be in order to be together."

"This all seems very deep. What do you think, in this ponder, would have happened, if we had got together years ago?"

"You mean if the stars had been in the right place, so to speak?"

"Yes."

"We were young, you were just about to get your degree, and I had just left school and was a bit young for my age, not very streetwise. We could have fallen for each other, leaving aside the bet. You would have gone on to do your PhD and it would have been a long-distance romance. Would it have lasted? Would we have married then? If we had had children would you have had to take any job to feed us and keep a roof over our heads? You didn't get married in the meantime, did you? So not being responsible for anyone else you were able to do what you wanted as far as your career went until you reached this point. I was able to build a career for myself until I reached a point where I could say 'This is not enough'. Did you find the same? If so at that point we met, clicked, and here we are. We are not the same people we were eighteen years ago."

"By hecky thump, and eeh ba gum," Ralph said, relapsing into Yorkshire vernacular. "That was a big ponder. I thought you didn't believe in astrology."

"I don't, I was only using that as an illustration."

"If we aren't the same people, we were eighteen years ago, who are we now?"

"Essentially the same but made different by our life experiences, grown and matured, I suppose and, hopefully, ready to meet again as who we are now and ready to put up with foibles which we might not have liked in each other when we were younger. Maybe we are nicer people than we would have been otherwise. Anyway, this is probably all nonsense."

"Maybe so," responded Ralph, "But I think you may have caught a grain of truth. I'm sure that some of my experiences have made me appreciate you more. You have certainly given me more than I had ever hoped to find in a relationship. Therefore I have changed since we met, and I feel as though I am a better person for knowing you."

"Wow," said Sally, "I feel that way about you even after such a short time, I know I feel as though I am a better person for knowing you. Somehow you seem to bring out the best in me. Perhaps if we stay together long enough and become even better, after forty years of marriage, say, we could be practically perfect."

After a moment, Sally said, "I've just had another thought."

"Yes, what's that?"

"You still haven't found a dragon to slay. When I get my energy back, let's go back to Cleckheaton and look for your dragon on Emley Moor."

Chapter 33

It was now nearly Christmas and Sally's illness had made everything very rushed. However, they did make it to the staff Christmas party again but decided to be very diplomatic and spent part of the evening with the library faction and the other part with the English brigade. Sally, of course, knew all the English staff to speak to if not well and in some instances knew more about their reading habits than they might have liked generally being known. On the other hand, it gave Ralph the opportunity of getting to know Sally's colleagues and discovered that they were a lot livelier than gossip about Librarians would have led him to believe. Although he had known Sally for nearly a year and had lived with her for four months, he should have realised that appearances can be deceptive.

After they arrived home from the Christmas party, Sally who was still not one hundred per cent fit, went straight to bed leaving Ralph downstairs. When he finally came to up to bed, he sat of the edge rather than getting undressed.

"Is everything all right?" he asked.

"Yes, why shouldn't it be?" Sally replied.

"Would you rather I slept in the other room?"

"No, don't be so daft. What's the matter?"

"I thought you were tired of me."

"What has brought this on?" she asked very concernedly.

"Well I know you've had this glandular fever, and I wondered if you were using it as an excuse to tell me kindly that you had had enough of me."

"Has this happened in the past? Don't answer that. I don't want to know what happened before you met me." She paused. "O my darling, surely you know me well enough by now to know that I can't be as subtle as that. If I want you to know something, I'll tell you straight out."

"But things have not been the same just recently."

"Surely that's in the nature of things. I was afraid that we would burn out, and the deathly passion that we had at first would fizzle out and die."

"I wanted to spoil you for any other man. I was jealous of any man whom you might meet in the future."

"I don't want any other man. You're more than enough for me. Come to bed and show me the man I want."

"You've been so ill I was frightened to touch you even. Will this be all right?"

"Let's give it a try and see how far we get," was the encouraging reply. "I'm afraid that my seduction techniques are non-existent otherwise I might not have been able to answer for the consequences sooner."

"You mean, you have been waiting for me to make a move?"

"I suppose I have. But I have only been feeling in the mood in the last few days. Do you know, I think that we really must talk more?"

He hurriedly got undressed and leapt into bed. He held her close to him and she put her arms around him and he knew that everything was going to be all right.

Sally awoke in the middle of the night to find that Ralph had an arm around her, clasping her so tightly to himself that he had wakened her. He was still fast asleep and obviously dreaming. She now had no fears that he did not enjoy her company and that he liked being with her. He was not going to let her go. Laughing quietly with delight to herself she tried to go back to sleep but the grip was so tight she could not relax, and it was a while before he stirred and released his hold.

The next morning, still lying in bed, they began to talk.

"You should never have agreed to marry me," said Ralph.

"I beg your pardon," responded Sally.

"I am not nearly good enough for you, you should be with someone else."

"Let's get one thing straight," Sally replied. "I know when I am well off, and I am well off with you. As far as I am aware there was no queue at the door of eager young men dying to ask me to marry them. There has only been you who looked at me and did not see a freak. How you work out that you are not good enough I don't know. You've looked after me superbly while I've been ill. Whatever you may think, I did not do it deliberately to give you the opportunity of getting out if you wanted to. If you remember I have given you several opportunities to change your mind. Why would I wait until now?"

"Now I know you better, I realise what a great girl you are, and I cannot believe, I still cannot believe, that you chose me."

"You'd better believe it, buddy. Once Sally Barton had made up her mind, it stays made up." Sally thought for a while and then said, "I've made mistakes in my life, I know I have. Perhaps I should have gone to university instead of getting a job, but I got a job, and I got a degree, and I got a professional qualification and a career such as it is so I don't regret not going to university sooner. I could have gone anywhere, Ormsbury was not on my list of preferred places to visit, but I have been very happy here and I've made some good friends. Then I met you. All right, we didn't have the greatest of starts but we got to know one another before things got serious, or at least I did. If we split up, it will have to be you, because I'm not going to. I am not going to regret the last few months. Why should I? They have been the best time of my life so far."

"I don't think that there is any answer to that. I now know where I stand."

"But do I know where I stand, or rather lie? You've been very good at telling me that I have made a mistake, now you tell me if you've made the mistake?"

"I haven't made a mistake. I love you. I want you. I enjoy living with you. I think about you all the time."

"Then what has this been all about?"

"I'm terrified of losing you. When you were ill, I had visions of you dying and I could not cope with the thought. I think I went onto autopilot for a while. So now you are better it seemed that if I told you to go, then I was in charge of your decision, and if I made it, you leaving wouldn't hurt so much."

She took him in her arms and held him tightly, "Don't be daft," she said, "I'm not going anywhere voluntarily. I'm with you forever, don't you forget it. I seem to remember I told you once before – don't make up my mind for me. I'm quite capable of making it up for myself."

They lay close together for a while. He put his arms around her and they just held each other for a long time. They were home.

Chapter 34

The year was coming to a close. Sally had not yet gone back to work, this was planned for the New Year, although she had made it to the Christmas Party, as she was still weak from the glandular fever. Although they were delighted at the progress that had been made in tracing the origins of George Ashcroft, they decided to leave the next part of the hunt until after Christmas. They hoped that by this time Sally would be truly back on her feet and back to work. The boredom was beginning to take its toll. There is nothing worse than waking up in the morning feeling full of beans and raring to go, climbing out of bed and discovering that it was taking all your energy to stand upright. Her mind was working well but she tired easily. As a result, they took up Les and Mag's invitation to spend Christmas with them in the Midlands. New Year was already arranged for Cleckheaton where Ralph's family and friends wanted to see him.

The drive down to Lineham was uneventful and they had a very pleasant time. Les and Ralph seemed to get on very well. The fact was that they both loved Sally and wanted the best for her. Les also enjoyed outdoor pursuits and in his youth had gone rock climbing. Soon the pair of them were discussing the best pitches, routes and the latest climbing gear. The holiday finished with Ralph promising to take Les the next time they went to the Lakes. This meant that a visit to Sally's little house was proposed for some time after Easter. Sally was just pleased that the two of them had got on so well.

Ralph and Sally set off for Cleckheaton on the day before New Year's Eve. Graham had invited them to a party on the night itself and Ralph thought that it would be a good move to invite Ria and her family over the day before for a meal, cooked, of course, by Sally. Sally could see that Ralph wanted to make amends to Ria and also to tell her all about the discoveries that they had made. He knew that she would not be pleased but hoped that she would at least listen to what he had to say before storming out and slamming the door.

In the event, it went much better than he had hoped. Sally stayed well out of the way in the kitchen preparing vegetables to go with the casserole she had made while Ralph told Ria about what they had found and the prospect of new relatives. Sally could hear voices from the living room but none were raised so she had hopes for a peaceful evening. After a while there was silence and the door opened and Ria came in.

"Is there anything I can do to help?" she said.

"No, but thanks for the offer, I think I've got everything under control," Sally replied.

"I'm afraid we didn't get off to a very good start when we last met," Ria responded.

"No, I think you thought I was a brainless bimbo, which I have never been taken for in my life it was quite refreshing."

"Can we start again?"

"Right, my name is Sally, and I'm a Librarian."

"My name is Ria, and I'm Ralph's sister, which probably makes me the guardian at the gate."

"You think he needs protecting?"

"To be honest I don't know. He never brought any of his girlfriend's back here once he went to university, so we thought, that is Mum and me, that he was ashamed of us."

"Oh, I don't think that was it at all. He told me once that he never felt confident about his girlfriend's making a good enough impression on your Mum to want them to face her scrutiny."

"It was all our fault?" Ria asked incredulously.

"Not really, I don't think so. Apparently, your mother had high standards and they were difficult to live up to."

"That's true. I had dreadful trouble getting them to agree to me marrying Alfie."

"On the other hand surely it made you even more determined and looked at him very carefully first."

"That's true. He's turned out to be a good one. But what about you? Ralph says he's going to marry you."

Sally laughed. "He keeps telling me that, and he has asked me and we're talking about Easter but we haven't done anything about it."

"How do you mean? I thought you were living together."

"We are, but he has put a condition on us actually getting married. He wants to know the answer to your mystery first. Anyway, we have just about got to the bottom of it so it could happen at any time."

After a pause, she added, "Your brother does like to know."

"How do you mean?"

"He seems to get an idea in his head and he must get to the bottom of it. He can and does make sense of the result, that's probably what makes him a good researcher. I'm the same. That might be why we get on so well. But it's a bit annoying when it gets in the way of your life."

"I think that you must be good for him, I haven't seen him so happy for a long time. I'm also pretty certain that Mum would have approved of you."

"That's very kind of you. He did say that of all his girlfriends I was the first that he would have considered bringing home to meet them. Anyway, I think the veggies are done so we can eat."

Graham's New Year Party in Cleckheaton went off with a bang. The weather being kind, and one and all had a good time.

The following day once they had emerged into the dawn of the New Year, Ralph and Sally began to consider their options for when Ralph began his new post at York University. They began to take stock and look at the house with a serious view to living there. They had decided to put Sally's house in Ormsbury on the market when they got back in the New Year. The housing market was beginning to move as people began to come to terms with the credit crunch but they had no idea until they had talked to an estate agent, as to how easy it would be to sell. They discussed the possibility of fitting all their belongings into one house and what they could get rid of and what they both most wanted to keep. Cleckheaton was within striking distance of York via the M62, M1 and the A64 and so could make a temporary base for them.

They still had not had the opportunity to go to look for the dragon on Emley Moor.

Chapter 35

Once they had returned to Ormsbury after the New Year celebrations they went back to the search for George Ashcroft. Because they had found the death notice in the paper, they now knew the names of the children of George and Beattie. Ralph's photograph was a clear identification as this photo had also appeared in the paper with an account of the accident. In this way, they knew that granddad George had a younger brother called John. Which made sense as Ralph's father was also John. Was Uncle John still alive? They looked in the phone book. There were about twenty J Ashcrofts listed and that only covered Ormsbury and the district to the South; the villages to the North were covered by a different book. Of these twenty only seven lived in the immediate area. Ralph got on the telephone and rang them all without result.

While Ralph was doing that Sally, who by now had gone back to work and was now much stronger and driving again, went up to Burscough Library to look in their phone book and came back with a further ten, all in the Burscough area.

"I did not realise how hard it was to try to track someone down," Ralph said.

By the time Ralph rang the ninth name on Sally's list he was beginning to despair. However, when the phone was answered by a female voice and he said for the sixteenth time, "I'm sorry to trouble you but I am trying to locate a gentleman called John Ashcroft who will be in his late seventies and whose parents were George and Beattie and he had a brother called George." He was unprepared for the reply.

There was silence at the other end of the phone and then the voice said, "Are you a reporter?"

"No."

"Are you trying to cause trouble?"

"No."

"Then why do you want to know?"

"I think I might be related to him."

"Oh."

"Have I got the right family?"

"Could be."

"Do you think it would be possible to come to see him?"

"He's not in good health and I won't have him troubled."

"If he's who I'm looking for I can give him some good news."

"You're not one of those Spiritualists, are you?"

"No."

"Well you can come next Saturday at 2.00 pm and I'll have my son here to make sure there's no funny business."

The following Saturday Ralph went alone to see John Ashcroft. He followed the directions to the address he had been given and found that it was a well looked after semi-detached house on a former council estate. The front garden and had been tidied for the winter, and the front door was fresh and modern. Despite the age of the occupants, someone was looking after the property well. He rang the doorbell. It was answered by an elderly lady of a little below average height which made her seem very small from Ralph's stature.

"Yes?" she said.

"I'm Ralph Armstrong," he introduced himself, "I've come to see Mr Ashcroft. I rang during the week and made an appointment."

"Mm. Are you sure you're not a reporter?" The lady asked.

"Who is it woman?" a male voice from the living room called. "Is that t'young lad as rang up?"

"Yes, Jack," she said. "It looks like t'young man."

"Well bring 'im in then. Let's see 'im then."

She showed Ralph into a neat and tidy living room. The furniture, though worn and had seen better days was of good quality and obviously intended to last. Although the furniture was stuck somewhere in the nineteen-seventies the décor was more modern with clean neutral paintwork and no wallpaper.

Sitting in an easy chair beside the fireplace was a little old man, but this was deceptive as he was sitting far back in the chair, which made him look smaller than he actually was. Ralph looked at him closely without seeming to do so but could see little resemblance to his father.

Ralph greeted him and shook his hand.

"Nah then lad what is't tha wants?"

"My name is Ralph Armstrong and I'm not a reporter, actually I'm a lecturer at the university, but I am trying to trace relatives of George Ashcroft who left here sometime in the 1950s. When I spoke to Mrs Ashcroft on the phone, I got the impression that you might be able to help."

"Well, I do have a brother, George, but we've not heard from him for nigh on fifty years. He could be dead by now for all I know."

"This might seem personal, but could I ask? Were your parents George and Beattie?"

"Yes."

"And were they killed in a motor accident in 1952 in Maghull?"

"Yes."

"Then you are the person I am looking for. I have to tell you that your brother, George, was my grandfather."

"How do you make that out?"

"It's a long story, and I'm not sure we've got to the end of it yet, but here goes. My father, John, said that his father, George, always said that the family, should never come to Ormsbury. Dad died about eight years ago and I got a job here and I thought that I would find out why. I always thought my surname was Armstrong, that's what it says on my birth certificate anyway, but we found out that George's name was really Ashcroft which gave us a starting point, so we started looking. Among the things I had found at my old home was an attaché case with old newspapers and a photograph in it. In one of the newspapers, there was an account of an accident when George and Beattie Ashcroft were killed. So, my girlfriend, Sally looked in the local paper and found that George had a brother. We looked in the 'phone book and tried all the J Ashcrofts until we found you."

"What made you think that he was connected to our George Ashcroft?"

"The photograph that was in the suitcase," answered Ralph, "It was of the same people that were in the accident. Sally took a photocopy from the microfilm at the library."

"Have you got the photograph with you?"

"No, I'm sorry, I was so anxious to get here on time I forgot it. Sally would have reminded me, but she's not been well and hasn't come today."

"I reckon that photograph is important," said John, "The day after Mam and Dad were found dead there were people in and out of the house all day. Our George came round for a few minutes. I do remember that, but he never came to the funeral, nor his Betty neither, which was odd because he was the eldest. There was another odd thing though. Later when things had settled down again, we could not find Mam and Dad's wedding photo which used to sit on the sideboard.

We thought one of the newspaper folks had taken it. We never tracked it down though."

"Can you remember what George was like?" asked Ralph.

"Well, he wasn't tall, not near as tall as you. You must take after your mother's family 'cos we're all about my height. But he was always cheerful. He had a really cheery smile. That's what I remember most. Made Mam laugh with his jokes, but he wasn't happy. He always wanted somm'at more. But that last day when he called round after the accident, he was white. I'd niver seen him so pale. All't colour had gone from him and Betty too. We niver thought we'd not see them again." John was saddened by the memory. "But you say he was your grandfather?"

"Yes, at least I think so," replied Ralph.

"Well, you do have a look of our George about you," said John.

"I never met him. He died when Dad was twelve. I remember Betty though. She died in 1996. I think she had had a hard life."

"How did George go?" asked John.

"He died in a trolley bus accident in Bradford, I'm not sure exactly what happened, like so many things in my family it wasn't really spoken of," replied Ralph.

"Where did he end up?" was John's next question.

"Over in Yorkshire, in a place called Cleckheaton. It's right by the M62 now but was a bit isolated then. It's not far from Bradford." was the answer.

"So I suppose you support Yorkshire for cricket then," said John the staunch Lancashire supporter.

"Yes I'm afraid so, but I could learn to appreciate Lancashire if it was essential."

"How come?" asked John.

"If I'm welcome to join the family," replied Ralph. "If you've no objection, I'll call again and bring the photograph. It might help to sort this out."

"Nay lad, you bring yon photo and we'll see."

"May I bring Sally as well? She's done all the work trying to trace my family. We still don't know why George and Betty left here and changed their name and I'd like to find that out."

"Mary, the young lad wants to come back again, and bring his lass and a photograph."

Mary came in from the kitchen. Her initial brusqueness had vanished as had the son who had gone out through the back door when he saw how well his father was getting on with the visitor.

"Very well," she said, "If you're not getting too tired with all this talk of the past."

"Nay," John said, "We've had a few mysteries of our own and this was one of them. It'd be grand to get to the bottom of at least one. Can you come again next Saturday?"

"I think that's OK. I'll have to check with Sally, but I'll let you know if there's a problem."

He rose, feeling a bit shaky. To have actually met a relative after all these years of not knowing about them was quite something. Sally would be fascinated. He knew she would be delighted to return with him the following Saturday. He said 'Goodbye' and left to drive back into Ormsbury.

When he got home, he told Sally all about the meeting.

"So that photograph, which you forgot to take, was really important, then?"

"That's right. Apparently, there was a photograph of the George and Beattie, his parents, a wedding photograph which used to sit on the sideboard of their home. After all the fuss had died down after the funeral, they found the photo of George and Beattie had disappeared, and I think the photograph that was in the suitcase is that photograph. I asked if I could go to see them again, and I can. If this is the same photograph then we have found George's family, my family!"

"But we still don't know why he left, and why he never came back, and not only that but said that your father and you, I suppose by inference, must never come back here either."

"That's true, but we are getting somewhere, thanks to you. Maybe we'll finally find out what it was all about. I've said, I'll take you next time to see them and perhaps they can tell us more."

Chapter 36

The following Saturday Ralph and Sally went back to Burscough. This time they had remembered the photograph. Once Mary had settled them in the front room, this time with cups of tea and biscuits, Ralph produced the photograph.

"Is this them?" said Ralph as he took the photograph, carefully wrapped in bubble wrap, out of the carrier bag.

"Ee lad," said John, "I niver thot to see this again. Mary come and have a look at this. This young man's brought Mam and Dad's picture back."

"How did you get that?" she demanded; she still was not sure about Ralph.

"I found it in a suitcase in the attic of my parent's house. He was called John Armstrong and I always thought his father was George Armstrong. I never knew him as he died when my father was about twelve years old. I was always told never to come to Ormsbury – but as you can see, I don't always do as I'm told."

"Son, if you're an Armstrong, why have you got a photograph of Ashcroft's?"

"I've only recently found out that my grandfather's real name was Ashcroft – he changed it but we don't know why."

Meanwhile, John had been looking at the photograph. "Good Lord," he said, "Mam and Dad. I niver thot I'd see this again. Mary put it on the sideboard. There now it looks just the way it used to. They niver had many photos taken and this were the best. You say it were in your attic. So what you are saying, lad, is you think our George is your granddad?"

"According to all the evidence we have found, yes, I'm beginning to think so," said Ralph, "but why did he leave here and change his name?"

"Well, he disappeared from here good and proper, no one could find him. We told the police but they niver came up wi' owt. He niver got in touch with us again and we niver heard owt about him from anyone. I think it had something to do with that court case."

"What court case?" asked Ralph.

"Them Kinsellas in Liverpool. That murder in Liverpool. He gave evidence."

"He gave evidence in the murder case?" asked Sally. "Don't you remember, Ralph, the other bunch of newspapers had a court case in them. I mean it was on the front page of 'The Echo', but we didn't realise it had anything to do with George or the family."

"I don't rightly know how George got himself involved," said John, "but he was right scared about it. I remember sitting on the stairs with him one night and him telling me that I was to look after Mam and Dad because he had to go to court and he didn't know what was going to happen. He looked right pale and really terrified. He thought he might've ended up in Walton Gaol. Betty was to go to her Mam if anything happened to him and take little John with her. But he came through that alright and then Mam and Dad were killed and George disappeared and we often puzzled about why. Then that daft fella came asking questions and stirring it all up again. But we could tell him nowt. He put it all in a book but I didn't believe it. He gave us a copy but it was so daft we threw it out."

"Can you remember his name?" asked Sally.

"Nay lass," replied John, "that's long gone. But I think it's t'only book written about it. There was no mystery about what happened. The only mystery was what happened to our George."

"Well, you have the photograph back, and I'm pretty certain you're my Great-Uncle and I've been able to tell you something about what happened to him. I have some old photographs at home of grandma and granddad which I'll look out for you. Then you'll be absolutely certain that I'm who I say I am," said Ralph.

"Nay, lad I'm sure you're George's grandson, no one else would come here with such a daft story. I believe you. But a photo of him would be grand to see, so you come again when you find it. Now then, how do you think Liverpool are going to do against United this season?"

Sally collected the cups and took the tray into the kitchen where Mary had hidden. She had not taken any part in the conversation but Sally knew that she had been listening keenly from the hallway.

"What do you think of all this?" asked Sally.

"I didn't want him upset," said Mary. "That author chap who wrote all that rubbish about George really unsettled John and he'd just come out of hospital after he'd had his knee done and didn't want to bother. Then he wrote all that rubbish about George and Beattie and the lad being murdered and John said he'd speak to no one else about it, so when your man rang, I thought it was another one. But it seems like it's all turned out for the best."

"This book said George, Beattie and John were dead?"

"Ay, what made him think that I don't know, but it right upset our John. He said if they were dead, he'd know like but of course, how could he. Turns out he was right all along."

"It looks as though that court case had something to do with George going away. We'll have to get hold of a copy of that book and see if we can find out more. I'm so grateful to you for letting us come. I know Ralph has been wanting to find answers to his questions for a long time but he couldn't do anything while his father was still alive. He died a couple of years ago so he has now been able to look into it."

"I must admit I was wondering why it had taken so long for a member of George's family to find us."

"You mean, you didn't think he was dead as well?"

"No. I remember George vaguely from my childhood. We lived next door to them. I went to school with John. It was devastating when his parents died. Then when George disappeared as well, we didn't know what to make of it. I'm so glad you've come now."

"We'll go in a few minutes."

"Come again. I can see that it's done John good. It seems as though as you get older things that happened when you were young become more important and I know that this is one of the things that has been troubling John. Another is, we never did find out who was driving the car that killed his parents that night. I don't suppose we'll find that out now."

After a few minutes, Sally went back into the living room, Ralph rose and took his leave and together they went home.

Chapter 37

Following their visit to see Uncle John Ashcroft and the information that he had given them about George's involvement in a court case, Sally and Ralph put their heads together and realising the importance of the newspapers, took a serious look at them. The newspapers contained the reporting of a murder trial. The defendant was Michael Kinsella, described as a notorious petty criminal, who had shot and killed a policeman during the attempted hijacking of a drugs consignment. This had taken place in the Dock Road area of Bootle in 1951. An unnamed accomplice had given evidence at the trial, had turning King's evidence, against his friends.

In order to find all the information they could, and to track down the book that John Ashcroft referred to, Sally looked up Kinsella on the internet and came up with a reference to a book called *Murder on the Dock Road and Other Crimes*, by Martin Smith. On checking Amazon and *abe.books*, she discovered that it was now out of print but had been published at least ten years ago.

Sally showed this information to Ralph.

"What do you want to do? Do you want to buy a copy of the book or borrow it from the library?" she asked.

"I think we'd better borrow it," replied Ralph, "particularly as John was so scathing about its truthfulness. When we know the truth maybe we'll write our own and put the record straight."

She put in a request for it at the local library, after finding that a copy was held in the system, and when the book came, they both read it avidly looking for clues. The greatest information they got was that the unnamed witness in the newspaper reports had been George Ashcroft whose identity had been suppressed to protect him. However the reported shout, by Michael Kinsella, from the dock after the verdict, "I know who you are and where you live. You'll be hearing from me again," had lent colour to the disappearance of George and his family. All attempts by the police, and the present author, Smith, had failed to find any trace of George, or his family. He had, therefore, reluctantly concluded that they had been murdered by some member of the Kinsella fraternity, and the bodies so well hidden, (he suggested them being dumped at sea in Liverpool Bay), that they would never be found.

Ralph and Sally both knew that this was not true but a further search of the internet revealed that Smith had died since the book had been published so there was no way they could set the record straight in that direction.

"What do you make of all this?" said Ralph, when they had finally got all the information together.

"It rather looks as though George really took fright when his parents were killed and disappeared from this neighbourhood for good. John said he had been white and terrified looking the last time that he saw him which was the day after the accident."

"The accident was only two days after the sentence was passed. He must have thought that there was a connection between the threat from the dock and the death of his parents, and just set off with his wife and my father and finished up, hidden, in Cleckheaton. I think I'd rather like to find out more about what George was really like."

"Your Uncle John is the first one to give us the time scale of George's disappearance," commented Sally. "So now we know when, and we think we know why. Perhaps you're right. If we found out more about George then we may begin to understand him."

"I wonder if we will ever get to know?" pondered Ralph.

"The only other thought is that if George was being threatened and was being hunted, they, whoever they were, never found him. There was nothing doubtful about the accident in which he died in Bradford, was there?"

"Don't start asking questions like that, or you'll have me looking over my shoulder all the time," responded Ralph.

"OK. He took fright, but there was actually nothing to be afraid of and left. He made a good life for himself, Betty and John and now we are here thinking about him. Good on you, George. It would be interesting to think what might have happened if he hadn't left. Anyway if he'd stayed, John would never have met your Mum and there wouldn't be 'a you' for me," finished Sally.

"I think you've had the last word this time," replied Ralph. "If it goes on like this, I shall have to think about having my revenge!"

Chapter 38

While he was looking through his own papers looking for some lecture notes Ralph found the missing copy of Sally's Richard III Magazine. He had been quite surprised because she was usually tidy as far as her society magazines were concerned and did not leave them lying around. He had idly picked it up and glanced through it and was surprised to see an article by Sally in it. He read and, as he knew very little about the subject, was very impressed. Because of her illness, he had not commented on it to her at the time, but one day in February when he noticed that the next issue of the magazine had come he said, "You didn't tell me that you wrote about Richard III?"

"O Lord," she said, "have I forgotten to put that away?"

"Why? Are you ashamed of it?" he asked.

"No." she replied. "But I did not want it marking by an expert, so I keep it quiet."

"You didn't want me to know?"

"Well, not really. You're an expert and I'm only an amateur. I just wanted to pretend that I knew what I was talking about."

"Look, Pet," he said, "I know very little about the Wars of the Roses, you're the expert as far as I'm concerned. You write what you like. I found the article before Christmas but didn't mention it then. Have you written another? I thought that the other article was very good. It was closely written and worth at least eleven out of ten for style and substance. I'll give you a pass mark any day."

"This is why I don't tell you. You're making fun of me."

"Yes, but only in the privacy of our own home."

"Well, please can we keep it that way?"

"Seriously, I'm very impressed. I wish you had told me sooner. I knew you read about Richard III but not that you researched him as well."

"Someone's got to do it. You know he didn't do it?"

"What?"

"Murder the princes in the Tower."

"Yes, I know."

"How do you know?"

"You've just told me."

"You're winding me up again, aren't you? Why did I ever get involved with a man like you?"

"You must have had a momentary aberration of the mind."

"I think it lasted a bit longer than a moment."

He caught her hand as she took the magazine from him. "Love, I'm only teasing," he said.

"I know," she replied, "But it's serious to me. I don't know why I let you wind me up so easily. No one else would get away with it."

"Look, what I have read is good. You make your point well. But why keep this talent hidden?"

"The staff at WLU terrify me sometimes with their erudition."

"Don't let that put you off, most of the time they are blowing in the wind, hoping to bluster their way into better positions. They probably know less than you about your subject. You are more closely involved with it than they are. They might disagree with you, but it is up to them to make their case not for you to give in."

"I suppose because I got my degree part-time, I thought that they would take me less seriously."

"Hell's bells, there is nothing wrong in doing anything part-time, particularly if it is something you love doing. You're more likely to get it right than they are."

"You do realise that you are putting your own profession down, don't you?"

"No, I'm just being realistic. It is not possible to know all about everything, but it is possible to know everything about a little and that is where the amateur comes in."

"Well, in that case, I have another confession for you. I wrote an article about the effigies in the Parish Church and it was published in a Heraldry magazine. It was quite well received."

"There you are then. For heaven's sake, my love, don't sell yourself short. Anyway when we've finally sorted Granddad George out perhaps you had better write it all out and put the record straight."

The next visit they made to see John Ashcroft was to meet the rest of the family. This was quite daunting for Ralph because they were all his relatives.

Mary made them very welcome and John's two sons were there together with his two sisters and their husbands. The aunts were delighted to meet Ralph and Sally and to hear from Ralph what had happened to their absent brother. After lunch, he said, "Could I ask you for your memories of George? I never knew him as he died before I was born. Also, my father was only about twelve when he died so he never knew him as an adult."

"I remember him coming home once in a really big flash car. I think it was American. I know he came to show Mum that he was doing well," said Lily the youngest sister, "I must have been about seven or eight at the time. I know the car didn't belong to him. I think he drove it for the man he worked for."

"I remember that," said June. "He let me sit in the front seat. I mean we were never allowed in the front seat of any car. Children always sat in the back."

"Yes, he let me too. Though we didn't go anywhere it was just parked outside. I think he was trying to impress the neighbours."

"That wouldn't have been difficult then. Most of us had nothing to start with, so that car was very grand."

"I knew he could drive because he drove a trolley bus in Bradford," said Ralph, "but he was a chauffeur?"

"I think he must have been," said John. "I know he did an apprenticeship in motor mechanics. He was very good at it. He could make a car sing."

"Dad said that he was useless with mechanical things and couldn't even mend his bike when the chain came off," said Ralph.

"Well, all I know is he was very good at it while he was living here," said John.

Ralph looked across at Sally to see if she had noted this titbit of information. She winked at him to show that she had heard.

"How do you think he got interested in big fast cars?" asked Ralph.

"Must've been those pictures," said John.

"What pictures?" said Ralph.

"Them gangster pictures he was always going to see."

"Oh, you mean the cinema."

"Yes, he was always going. We had two cinemas here then and he would go every night if he could. He used to take me sometimes, but mostly he went with his mates, or on his own. I didn't like them as much as I liked the westerns. The lone outlaw trying to be good and shooting up even worse than the baddies. They don't make films like them these days. But gangster movies, that were George's thing. Shoot outs in the mean streets. James Cagney falling off the top of buildings saying, 'Top of the world, Ma', he took me to that one. Then when he was about eighteen, he started going into Liverpool of a Friday and Saturday evenings and we never knew what he got up to."

"My brother, Harry, saw him in the Golden Lion one Saturday talking to some really flash guy," said Lily's husband Jim. "He asked the barman who it was but the barman said, 'Don't ask questions, you're better off not knowing.'"

"You never told me that," said Lily.

"It didn't seem important at the time, and Harry only told me about it much later. In fact, I think it was after the accident when George disappeared but he had seen him years before."

Ralph was beginning to get a picture of George and could see how he might have got mixed up with criminals. This visit had given him so much to think about and he felt very grateful to John and Mary for letting Sally and himself come and meet the family. John's sons were equally intrigued to discover that they had an uncle who was, at the very least, on the fringes of gangland.

"Were there a lot of criminals in Liverpool after the war?" asked Ralph.

"I suppose there must have been," said Jim, "it was a thriving port with ships coming and going all the time with plenty of opportunities for thieving and the black market. There was still rationing remember, until about 1954. So there was a ready market for anything extra."

Mary who had been sitting quietly knew that after all this reminiscing it would take John some time to come back from the past decided to change the subject.

"How are you feeling now?" she said, turning to Sally.

"I'm coming along," said Sally, "but it takes time. I've been back to work since January but I'm still having days when I've not got much energy. But according to the doctor, I'm going to be like that for several months yet. You're not supposed to get it when you're in your thirties."

"Sally's been very ill," said Mary to the rest of the room. "Any road, love, I'm glad to hear you're getting better."

"Well, Ralph has been looking after me really well, so I can sing the praises of the men in your family," replied Sally.

"Nay, lass," said John, "don't say things like that. Ashcroft men tend to be a bit old fashioned."

"Dad, if our Ivy could hear you say that," said John's son Eric, "she'd murder you."

"I heard that, Dad," a voice came from the kitchen, "Haven't you heard of the new man, who can do everything a woman can except give birth."

"I think, John, you had better say no more before you get into real trouble," said Mary. John mumbled a bit but said no more.

After a little while longer, Sally began to feel tired and asked Ralph if they could go home.

When they got home Ralph made some drinks and they sat thinking about what they had heard.

"So, George was a very good motor mechanic, who drove a big flash car for a criminal in Liverpool," said Ralph after a while. "That explains how he got mixed up in the Kinsella murder case. I bet he drove for Michael Kinsella. I can see that being a getaway driver would appeal to him."

"We don't know that for sure," said Sally, "we're only putting two and two together. We might be making five. But it certainly fits what we know so far. He was driving the van when the policeman was shot. He was a witness at the trial. It never said how involved he was with them. Had he been working for Kinsella or only brought in on that one occasion? I think I'm going to have to read the book and the newspapers accounts again."

Chapter 39

It was now drawing towards the end of the Spring Term and the date that they had thought about arranging for their wedding. Ralph had made enquiries at the Register Office in Ormsbury and together they had booked it and Room 47 for a small reception afterwards. The term would have finished by then as Easter was only another two weeks away. They had decided on a Friday as there was still a vacancy in the timetable and availability at the venue. Sally had bought a new dress and shoes and booked an appointment at the hairdressers. Lynne was going to be her witness and Graham; Ralph's old school friend was going to be his. They had sent out the invitations and everyone was able to come. Les was going to escort Sally as he was only too glad to give her away, he said.

Friday 31 March dawned bright and clear, without a cloud in the sky and was also unusually warm for March. By mid-morning Sally was ready in her new dress and had been to the hairdressers and was looking almost beautiful even to her own critical eye. The guests were beginning to arrive, most notably her brother Les and his family. Les had been home on leave which was a marvellous coincidence.

At 11.30, they made a move towards the Register Office crammed into two cars. They managed to climb out without too much loss of dignity and Sally was able to shake herself into shape. "Remind me to have my own car next time I get married," she thought as they went through the door into the lobby. Here Ralph and Graham were waiting. Also waiting to greet them were Ria and Alfie and their children who had come over from Cleckheaton and John and Mary who had come down from Burscough.

The actual ceremony was over so quickly that Sally felt like asking for a replay in order to appreciate it more. She was kissed by Ralph and all the guests and then they had to leave as another wedding party was due.

Outside, Ralph had ordered a car to take both Sally and himself to the restaurant while the rest of the party had to make their own way. Les had already parked his car in the restaurant car park so knew where they were going, and at 12.00 noon, they all entered the restaurant in a happy excited melee. Once again, Ralph had taken charge and they were greeted with glasses of champagne and fruit juice for the children. The meal passed off in a happy babble of noise and then there was a cry of 'Speech, speech'. The other diners were rather amused at what was going on but no one actually complained about the noise.

Ralph rose. "In the absence of a best man, because as you all know, I am the best man here." Cries of 'sit down', and 'rubbish'. "I will make this speech to thank you all for coming and to introduce my wife to you. Formerly known as Sally Barton, we now know that she is really Sally Armstrong; her secret is now out." Cries of 'Nonsense' and 'We knew her first', and 'I've known her longer than you.'

"I will not be put off," continued Ralph, "When I came here nearly two years ago little did, I think that within a year I would have fallen in love and with a Librarian. Librarians aren't married, they don't get married, they are frosty spinsters wearing pince-nez telling you that they have no 'love' under the counter, and to be quiet, 'Silence' being their watchword. But in the last year, I have received a culture shock, none of that is true. Librarians are wonderful, in fact, I recommend that every home should have one. In fact, gentlemen, if you haven't got one in your family already go out and find one now, immediately, this instant your life will be vastly improved." He sat down with a thud. Then stood up again. "I forgot, ladies and gentlemen a toast, to Sally, my lovely, wonderful wife." The assembly shouted "Sally" and drank her toast.

Again the cry went up "Speech". This time Sally stood.

"Ladies and gentlemen," she began, "In the absence of a father of the bride you've got me. This time last year my life was continuing on its normal tranquil path towards old age and oblivion when an Anglo Saxon strode into view. Now we all know about Anglo Saxons don't we, they are the ones who came and saw and conquered but a bit later than Julius Caesar. Their most famous son was Alfred the Great, well I would like to introduce you to Ralph Strongarm, the latest in a long line of Anglo-Saxon heroes. Well, at least he's a hero to me. I mean he would have to be a hero to put up with me." Cries of 'rubbish'. "I would like you to drink to the health of my hero husband, a word I am going to have to get used to from now on, Ralph Armstrong. Ralph." The assembly cried "Ralph" and drank the toast.

At 2.30 pm, the restaurant closed and the party had to leave. The mood was such that no one wanted to break up the celebration so it was decided that they would all go down to Sally's house and continue it there. Fortunately, while the mood was elated two members of the party had drunk nothing other than a sip of champagne and so were able to drive the short distance round the one-way system back to Sally's house. Once they arrived, they spilt into the house and over-spilled into the backyard as it was a bit crowded. The kettle was put on and bottles were opened and a long lazy afternoon was begun. Sally took her niece and nephew to the park to fly a kite for an hour to work off some of their energy until Ralph came looking for them.

"Come on home," he said, "we're missing you."

"I know," she replied, "but the kids were getting bored so I brought them here while the rest of you sorted yourselves out."

"I think they have all found corners now," he said, "and the children look tired, come back now. Besides I'm missing you. The bride can't go missing on her wedding day."

"True that would be too much good luck for the groom," she replied. "O Lord, I am tired too. Come on you two," to the children, "we're going back now."

They packed up the kite and walked back to the house, the children dancing ahead and with Ralph and Sally holding hands.

"What's everyone doing?" Sally asked.

"Les and Mags are asleep on the sun loungers in the back yard, Graham is trying to pick up the Yorkshire Cricket match on the radio (would you believe it the cricket season's started). Mary is prowling your bookshelves and squeaking, Lynne made tea for anyone who wanted it and is washing up and Pam is investigating the fridge-freezer to see if there is anything for tea. Ria and Alfie decided to head back home as the children were a bit fractious and I was totally superfluous to requirements so I thought I'd come and look for you."

"What a good idea."

At that moment a small voice said, "Uncle Ralph my legs are tired can I have a piggyback?" Ralph bent down and hoisted Jen onto his back. "Wow, its high up here," she said.

"Are you all right up there?" asked Sally.

"Oh, yes," said Jen. "It's like being in a helicopter."

So they walked back to the house. Sally wondered if Ralph realised how domesticated they both looked, Ralph piggybacking Jen and James holding Sally's hand. James began to lag a bit. He too was getting tired but was too big to carry.

"Come along, Sprig," she said.

"Why do you always call me Sprig, Aunty Sally?" he asked.

"Because you are a sprig, or maybe a twig. Which would you like to be?"

"What's the difference?"

"Not a lot really."

"I'll be a sprig then. What's a sprig?"

Sally pulled a small cutting sized piece from one of the shrubs as they passed. "This is a sprig," she said.

"So it's off a tree. I'm not off a tree."

"Ah, but you are," Sally replied. "You're a sprig on a branch of the old family tree."

"What's a family tree?"

"It's when you can trace your ancestors back to a proto-plasmodial amoeba in the primordial sludge from which we have all come."

"What's a proto-plasmodial amoeba, Aunty Sally?"

Sally laughed. "I asked for that. I'll tell you the answer to that another day when you remember to ask me," she said.

As they neared the house she said, "Let's give them another hour, then some tea and cake, and tell them it's time to go home."

"Good idea, can we kick them out?"

"Why not, it's our wedding."

"Did you say cake!"

"Yes, I bought a small wedding cake. Oh Lord, it's in the boot of your car, I thought we might need it at the restaurant. Mind you it is in a cool bag so it should be all right. Will you get it out?"

"Will do as soon as I lose the child hanging around my neck, she's strangling me. The cake arriving might concentrate people's minds."

They went into the house.

Chapter 40

The next day, they set off on their honeymoon and as they were driving towards Newhaven to get the ferry to France, Sally, remembering what Lynne had said about Ralph asking her to marry him and when they stopped a Motorway Service Area she decided to take the bull by the horns and said, "Now that we are safely married do you think you could tell me what made you ask me?"

"You don't give a man much chance to come up with a clever answer, do you?" was the response.

"I only want the truth," she said.

"Well, I fancied you, in fact, I fancied you a lot, and then when Mary suggested I ask you to help with my mystery, I thought it was a heaven-sent opportunity to get to know you better. And I did. Get to know you better. Then when you came with me to Cleckheaton and we found out that our family name wasn't Armstrong I was knocked sideways because I thought I knew all about my family, all right there was the mystery bit, but everything else was true. I had found that nothing was true, and for a little while, I felt as though I had lost my identity. At least it felt like it. You were so concerned for *me* and made sure I was all right, and I knew then that I wanted you on my side. You told me nothing had changed. I was who I always had been, and Graham told me not to be so daft and I realised what a lovely, caring person you are, didn't anyone ever tell you that?"

"Yes, they have, but usually in the context of 'You'll make someone a really good mother'. The only problem is that you have to find a man to provide the child first. And men don't, didn't, find me attractive enough to want to go that far. Mind you they probably weren't looking for mothers themselves."

"Well, their loss is my gain. I don't want you as a mother, but as a partner and lover, both of which you are very good at."

"Thank you, kind sir."

"I am so glad you said 'yes'. For once I am really looking forward to the future now, I've got you. Right, this is getting far too serious. I did have another reason for wanting to marry you," he continued as they got back into the car to head back onto the motorway.

"Go on," said Sally very warily.

"I am really, really dying to know all about the Dewey Decimal Classification System and I thought that if we were married you might not kill me after you told all!"

Sally started to laugh, she laughed out loud and almost hysterically.

"You've got to stop the car," she said, "otherwise I won't answer for consequences."

Ralph pulled into the side of the road and brought the car to a stop. Sally threw her arms around him and gave him a big, passionate kiss.

"You are mad, you know that, don't you? Oh, I do love you so very much. You make me laugh and don't treat me like 'the little woman' that needs to be patronized. You treat me as an adult human being, I feel safe with you, and I love you for that. I think the future looks great too."

"I hope you don't feel too safe with me. I rather fancy myself as being a bit risky and spontaneous who elopes with the first willing accomplice."

"That's OK, I'll risk that too. I rather like that side of you. It means that I don't know what is going to happen next. It's all an adventure for me. By the way, what is going to happen next? You haven't told me where we are going?"

"We are going to France and I am not telling you any more than that. Let's get going we've sat here long enough." He started the engine put the car into gear and set off for Newhaven.

Chapter 41

The ferry left promptly at 12 noon and docked on time at 18.30 in Dieppe. It had been an uneventful crossing but Ralph would still not tell Sally where they were heading. They had lunch on board but were ready for another meal by the time they disembarked. Ralph drove very carefully, getting used to the opposite side of the road problems encountered when first arriving in another country in a familiar car. However, it soon became apparent that Ralph had been here before and knew his way around. They stopped at a small restaurant and had dinner and then set off again for the short drive to the hotel on the outskirts of Rouen. Sally was totally bemused by this.

"Why are we in France?" she asked, "I don't know where I thought we were going, but Rouen?"

"I was going to keep quiet," Ralph replied, "but I can see that I am not going to get any peace and quiet until I tell you. A little bird told me that you have always wanted to go to Chateau Gaillard and that is where we are going, but it is too far to go all at once so we are stopping near Rouen for the night."

"Wow!" said Sally, "I shall have to have a word with the little bird. Yes, I have always wanted to go but this is too much. I know I said that I wanted adventures but that was because I wanted to have them with you, and by going to places you wanted to go to. Do you really want to go too?"

"I must admit that I have been before, but that doesn't mean that I don't want to take you. Besides, it was quite a while ago, and, who knows, we might get lost which could be an adventure in itself. Anyway, we are staying the night in Rouen and going to the cathedral in the morning before going on."

They found the small hotel that Ralph had chosen quite easily as it was one that he had stayed in before.

"Have you brought any of your girlfriends here?" Sally asked when had reached their room.

"No," replied Ralph. "Look, Sally, you know I have had other relationships but none of them compare to what you and I have. I would not jeopardize this for anything."

"I'm sorry," said Sally, "it's just that I cannot believe that you would want to marry me and I can't help feeling a bit overawed and just hope that I am not second best. I know we've been together now for a while but I still can't believe that it is true."

"In no way are you second best, in fact, you are the best thing to ever happen to me. Any other girlfriends I might have had are gone, in the past, I regret none of them. You are the one for me. *Numero uno, primo superbo*."

Sally laughed. "I didn't know you could speak Italian."

"I don't. It's just that when I was at the High School, they took a party to Italy to show us the Renaissance and Rome. One of the guides, who actually spoke excellent English used to emphasise the importance of the artist by saying something similar, so that the gang of us used to use it to describe anything cool, or gross, or whatever the latest buzz word was when we came back. It just came back to me now and it seemed appropriate."

"Thank you for that."

"We shall always be honest with each other. No games. I know that we've been living together, but somehow this seems very special having made the commitment."

"I'd like that. I promise to always tell you the truth about how I feel, as long as you do the same. That doesn't mean that we have to tell each other everything, but only the important things like, why do you always squeeze the toothpaste from the wrong end of the tube, always leave the toilet seat up and, why don't you hang the towels up in the bathroom."

"And like, why do you always tell me dinner will be ready in five minutes and it's ready in two, so I am always in the wrong place. Five minutes is time to do a job, two minutes isn't. Also please don't start to nag, you haven't up to now so please don't start. My mother never nagged Dad and they got on just fine. Apart from that, you are perfect. I shall have to improve, I can see."

"Don't try too hard I don't really want to change you, we'll just find a way of living, and from now on dinner will always be ready 'now' when you ask. I also solemnly promise never to nag. If I ask once and it isn't done, I'll do it myself. Remember before I met you, I was an independent woman who had to get everything done by herself."

"So we go on as we are and we'll mould into one another without noticing the change."

"Starting from the day you asked me to marry you at the Orphans' Picnic, anything that happened to either of us before we met has no bearing on us now. The past is the past, it has made us who we are now and I will not bring it up again. If there is something you want to discuss that's fine but the future is what is important."

He drew her towards him and held her close, "That is all I want," he said, "you and the future." After a few minutes of silence, while they just held each other, he added, "I think this is going to work."

"It won't fail for lack of trying," Sally replied into his chest.

"The honeymoon starts here," Ralph said.

"What have we been doing up to now?" Sally asked.

"That was just practice," said Ralph.

They went to bed.

Chapter 42

The next day after a visit to Rouen Cathedral to see where Richard I's heart was buried, they set off to Les Andelys driving on the winding road that for part of the time runs along beside the Seine. From here they could begin to see the towering ruin of Chateau Gaillard in the distance and could appreciate the magnificent setting of Richard I's castle as they neared the river.

Ralph had booked a room in a small hotel near the Seine which had particularly fine views of the Chateau which he knew would be appreciated by his wife. Sally could only stand, a little in awe, with the knowledge that she had finally arrived at the site of one of her favourite ruins. She could hardly wait to walk up to the castle and look around, but wait she did. Tomorrow would do.

The next day they bought the makings of a picnic in the town and then strolled, hand-in-hand, around the ruins which lived up to Sally's expectation of them. She enjoyed working out the ground plan and looking for those vital pieces of architecture without which no castle is complete, the garderobes. The disposal of sewage was an important element in castle construction, as it helped to cut down disease during a siege and for some reason, Sally felt that this had been an under-researched element in medieval buildings. Ralph would have to get used to this. That and the position of water storage tanks, or cisterns, always played a part in Sally's exploration of any new ruin.

After a while, they found a stone block and sat down.

"Has this lived up to expectation?" asked Ralph.

"Oh, yes," replied Sally. She was almost speechless as she looked around her. "This was an amazing idea of yours to bring me here. Thank you so much." She put her arms around his neck and gave him a kiss.

"Steady on," said Ralph, "it's only a building. Actually, it's even less than that it's only a ruin, and when you've seen…"

"One ruin you've seen them all," finished Sally. "That is not quite true. This is a Norman fortress built by Richard I, our Richard I, to protect the eastern borders of Normandy. So it is English in that sense, and there aren't many of those in France. It was built at the time of the crusades and if you can't get to the Holy Land this is the next best thing." She paused and then said, "What are the plans after this?"

"I thought we might go to Honfleur and look at the medieval wooden church, and then perhaps, Caen, and Bayeux before going to Cherbourg to get the ferry back to Southampton."

"Is any of that booked or paid or can it be changed?"

"Yes, nothing is set in stone, even the ferry isn't booked. We will just have to take potluck to get back. To be honest, I hadn't thought much beyond getting here. When I travel, I usually just wander."

"That's all right. I just wondered. Would you mind if we stopped here for a couple of days and then get the ferry back from Le Havre?"

"No, if that is what you want to do."

"I'm just thinking that it would be nice (what a useless word) just to potter and get to know one another. I still have tired spells following my illness so it would be nice to just drift after all the travelling. I have to go back to work on Tuesday after Easter. Please could we just stay here and get to know one another? This is supposed to be our honeymoon and now I don't feel like rushing around anywhere anymore. Would you mind?"

"That sounds good to me. I'll see if I can book us on the night ferry on Friday, but we can stay here until then." Ralph took out his mobile phone and selected the ferry line number and booked the return sailing on the night crossing on Friday. "All done," he said at the end of the call, "we have only to check with the hotel and we are here until Friday."

By this time Ralph was sitting on the grass and leaning against the stone block. Sally slid off the block and onto the grass beside him. He put his arm around her and they sat comfortably together looking at the view. After a while, they unpacked the picnic and had lunch. The sun moved round and their corner took on a chill as a wind came off the river and they got up and made their way back down into the town to their hotel.

That night after they had gone to their room Sally said, "I want to say thank you again for today, it has been magical and I'll never forget it. I am so lucky to have found you."

"Au contraire, madam," replied Ralph, "I'm the lucky one, and as I came to Ormsbury looking for why I should not go there, I think I did the finding."

"Well, either way," said Sally, "I'm going to show you how I say thank you."

And she did.

The last few days of the holiday went past at a gentle pace and both of them knew that once they were back home their normal busy lifestyle would take over and so they made the best of the short time they had together. They talked of this and that, walking by the river and solved a few inconsequential problems. Although they had been living together for some months and had got to know each other quite well in that time, Sally had been ill and Ralph had been troubled by his mystery which was now almost solved. As a result, they could look forward to a life together where all the major problems had been solved. The next few months would see them move to Cleckheaton. Sally's house was going to be put on the market when they got back to Ormsbury. They had been reluctant to do it before because Sally had been so ill and because they did not want to end up living out of suitcases if the house had sold quickly. Now they realised that that was unlikely to happen so they were considering letting it if there were no buyers in the offing.

Chapter 43

Traditionally when a man married, he provided his wife with a house, and he carried her over the threshold to begin her new life. The Bride's job was to turn that house into a welcoming home. In modern times so many single people either rent or buy their own home so that when they marry, there are two homes to turn or amalgamate into one. Ralph's house was miles away and had played no part in the initial setting up of their home together. He had already lived in the house sometime so there was little to do when they returned to Ormsbury.

Ralph had brought one box home from his study at the university at the end of the previous term and it was left sitting on the living room floor. How no one had fallen over it during the wedding festivities no one was quite sure. It had obviously got mixed up with the wrapping paper and the presents. Sally opened it. It was full of mugs. Dirty Mugs.

"Ralph, you'd better come and have a look at this," said Sally as she carried the box into the kitchen.

Ralph got up from the settee and followed Sally into the kitchen.

"I think we'd better wash these before going to bed," said Sally. "Do you want to wash or dry?"

"I think I'd better dry," was the reply, "I don't want dishpan hands." She hit him with the tea towel.

Several sinks full of water later Sally said, "Where on earth did all these manky mugs come from?"

"Ah, well, actually they're mine," replied Ralph, "I keep them at work so that I can give my students a drink during seminars."

"And you let them get into this state?"

"I bring them home at the end of each term and give them a wash. I tried to do it last time without letting you know, but this time you've found out my deep dark secret."

"How many students actually drink out of them?"

"The boys do, the girls tend to refuse."

"Do you wonder why? I'm surprised you haven't been prosecuted for endangering life. These could do with a good soak."

"I know, but what in?"

"Bleach. Did your mother never tell you that?"

"I don't think I was listening. Did you know we have forty-two mugs between us?"

"Forty-two, eh. Isn't that the answer to life the universe and everything?"

"Yes. You mean here in this kitchen we have the answer!!!" They both started to laugh. They were so tired that hysteria was not far behind, but common sense took over and Sally put bleach in the washing up bowl and added water and all the stained mugs to steep until morning. She then went up for her bath.

Later when Ralph came into the bedroom after having his bath Sally said, "I've got a sort of confession to make."

"How do you mean 'a sort of confession'?"

"Well, it's something I said last year which might come back to haunt me."

"Go on."

"There was a bit of a do in the SCR, I think the Vice-Chancellor was thanking everybody for all the hard work they had put in during the year and senior admin staff had been invited. One of the girls in the group asked me how I liked living on my own. (I later found out she was planning to buy her own house), and I said that I didn't mind being on my own but it would be nicer if I had company."

"This will haunt you, why?"

"Because someone might tell you this in the context of 'Sally didn't like living alone and she only got married for companionship'"

"Ah, I see your problem."

"However, I can assure you that I did not marry you for companionship I married you because I love you, besides, I'm not that cold-blooded."

"I know."

"You know what?"

"That you aren't cold-blooded, in fact, you are very hot-blooded, and I think you are enjoying yourself hugely, so if anyone says anything I shall just smile and say, 'thank you for telling me' and let them think what they like."

"I don't care about them, it was you I wanted to know the truth."

"I know we've only been together for a short while, but if this is companionship let's have more of it. Now shut up and let's get some sleep, it's nearly midnight and it could be another long day tomorrow."

Chapter 44

One day towards the end of April, Ralph came home from WLU with something to tell Sally.

"Do you remember Tom Williams?" he said. "He was one of the lads at Ambleside and you put him down. I think you called him the terror of the Lower Fourth."

"I remember," she replied. "I was rather harsh on him. Particularly now we've found out we all knew each other at Leeds, or at least in the Brotherton. Why what's happened?"

"He wants to come to visit. Apparently, he's in Manchester on business next week, and wonders if we can put him up for the night. I rather got the feeling that he wants to talk to me about something."

"I can't see a problem. Which night?"

"I think Tuesday."

"That's OK. If you two want to talk I'll go over to Pam's for an hour. I'm sure she said she had got a bottle in."

"You won't need to go out."

"I'd better if he wants to talk to you. It'll be best if I'm out of the way."

"But we'll have a meal first?"

"Yes, I can rustle something up out of my vast repertoire of culinary disasters, mind you they always taste better if you help."

"Are you flattering me?"

"You should be so lucky, it's just that you are a better cook than I am. Of course, tell him to come as early as he can and we'll make him welcome."

"But I thought you couldn't stand him."

"Only when he was being condescending and rude to me."

The following week Tom arrived at about 6.30 pm having driven over from Manchester. He brought his bag in and Sally showed him to the rather cramped spare room. There was room for the spare single bed and somewhere to lay out his clothes. It was where the niece and nephew slept when they came to stay. When he had freshened up, he came downstairs to Sally's pasta with ragout sauce meal which was one of her specialities. They opened a bottle of wine and the evening got off to a good start. There was a bit of a strained atmosphere for a while and they realised, that when Sally asked after Tom's family, that Tom did not want to talk about personal matters so early in the evening. Maybe this was what he wanted to discuss with Ralph. What he did say though was startling.

"Do you know, ever since we were all at Ambleside, and we talked about Leeds, I got to thinking about those days and, for some reason, Sarah Brown popped into my head. Do you remember her Ralph?"

"It's funny you should say that, because she came up in conversation not so long ago, in fact, I found a photograph of her. You remember that last day when we dragged her out of the Brotherton. What made you think of her?"

"I don't really know. I've been thinking about the past quite a bit lately, I'll tell you why later, but I remembered our bet with you. You could not get her to go out with you no matter how many times you asked her."

"Or tried to ask her," laughed Ralph, "it was a total no, no. She must have seen right through me."

All through this conversation, Sally kept quiet wondering where it was leading.

"She was a very perceptive young lady, and so young. I wonder whatever happened to her? Sally, do you remember a Sarah Brown at the Brotherton? If you were there when we were you must have known her?"

"I'm sorry, I don't remember a Sarah Brown. There was a Sarah Harrison and me Sarah Barton but no Sarah Brown. That I would have remembered."

"Perhaps we got the name wrong, then. Anyway, I just wondered what happened to her."

"Until we get the right name, we'll never know," said Ralph, giving Sally a wink as she leaned over him to collect his empty plate.

"Thank you, Sally, that was really tasty," said Tom, as he handed her his empty plate, "I don't often get the chance of a homecooked meal. Forget about the washing up, we'll do it."

"Are you volunteering me?" said Ralph.

"Sorry, and in your own home too. I'm all over the place at the moment."

"I'm going to leave you with the dessert, another of my specialities, lemon meringue pie, as I'm going out to let you two catch up on your boy's talk. I'm going to see a friend."

As she leaned over Ralph to kiss him 'Goodbye', she said. "Are you going to tell him about Sally Brown?"

"I might save that for later," he replied.

She poked her head back into the room and said, "I'll see you both later," and off she went.

"Right," said Ralph opening bottles of beer, there had been wine with the meal but beer goes better with a chat. "What did you want to talk about?"

"It's this credit crunch, I've lost my job, that's why I came up to Manchester for an interview. My wife is threatening to leave if I don't find one soon, and she's told me our eldest might not be mine. In fact, it's a hell of a mess. I think that's why I started thinking about the good old days when we were young and life was simple."

"I don't think life was ever really simple, it just seems simple now because it's got so complicated since."

"Your life doesn't look complicated to me."

"That's because you're not living it. My job here is only temporary and finishes at the end of this term. I've got another one in York starting next autumn but we will have to up sticks and move back to Yorkshire. As you can see the house is up for sale. With house prices being what they are, we can't guarantee that we will be able to afford to find somewhere to live. My old home in Cleckheaton is still ours and we could live there but it's not ideal. I could commute but Sally would not be able to get another job until we are settled. Anyway, that's my moan."

"I can see we all have problems. Grace really hit me with this one. I thought she would support me but all she does is moan about where the money going to come from and we're going through our savings, which weren't big to start with, as though there's no tomorrow. Then she decides to tell me our marriage is a sham because she thinks Oliver could be someone else's. I know she was seeing someone else when we first met, but, when she told me she was pregnant, I was the sap who proposed. Apparently, the other one told her it was her problem and walked away. In fact, I'm at the end of my tether. I'm sorry to burden you with my problems but you always seemed so together I thought I'd run them past you to see if you had any solutions."

"Thanks for the vote of confidence. I may have seemed in control but that was because nine-tenths of the time I had no idea what was going on. Sally's the one with the ideas. She can spot a flaw in your reasoning at twenty paces. If you like, I'll put it to her when she gets back and see what she thinks, she won't come up with a solution straight away, and of course, she doesn't know Grace, but she'll think of something."

After getting the problems off his chest, Tom transferred his interest to the current football season and reason went out of the window. At 10.30, he said that he would have to be going to bed but before he went, Ralph said, "Sally said I was to tell you that I did win that bet all those years ago."

"How do you mean? Sarah Brown actually went out with you?"

"Yes. In fact, rather more than that. She's married me."

Tim stood stunned for a few moments. "So Sally is Sarah Brown. I wonder if I subconsciously recognised her, and that's what made me start to think about those days. How did you find out?"

"The photograph I found, the one I told you about. When I looked at it, I recognised her on it. She did not recognise me because if you remember I grew my hair long that summer and I had not had it cut for about nine months but had had it done that morning. She never knew that it was me."

Tim reached into his pocket for his wallet. "A Williams always pays his dues," he said.

"Not acceptable, out of time," replied Ralph. "Besides, your need is greater than mine at the moment. If I'm ever on the breadline I'll come and collect. Goodnight Tom, see you in the morning."

When Sally came back about half an hour later, she found Ralph busy catching up with washing the dishes which had been left unwashed in the sink since she went out. She joined him at the sink and the pots were soon washed and put away.

"I gather the washing up came a poor second to a good chat," she said.

"Yes, Poor Tim, he has got problems." Ralph quickly told Sally Tom's dilemma and her response was as he expected.

"I don't know where you get the idea that I can solve everybody's problems from," she said. "You know I can't."

"But you have a practical approach to things, and we seem to manage to work out our problems."

"I know, but that's us. Other people think differently."

"You can put the female point of view, though, can't you?" he cajoled.

"You're a great flatterer. I wish I'd known this about you sooner. I might not have got involved. Let me think about it, and we'll talk in the morning," she said as they went upstairs.

The next morning, Sally woke early as she usually did when she had something on her mind. She hated being asked for advice and, as far as her tongue would let her, never gave it unless asked for. Sometimes her tongue jumped in before her brain got into gear. She thought she had something that she could say on the subject but was not looking forward to saying it.

Over breakfast, Tom asked, "Have you got any advice for me?"

"Actually, I don't like giving advice," she replied, "but here are a couple of suggestions which you could think about. Have you talked to Grace? Does she know how you feel about things? Have you asked her what she thinks about the situation? Have you listened to her? Don't say anything to Oliver. As far as he is concerned, you're his father, don't take that away from him. If there's a problem financially, and the children have to make do with less, explain it to them, not in detail, you'll know what to say. I didn't mean to say all this. Just talk it through with Grace."

"You have been thinking about it, haven't you?" Tim commented.

"She does think about things, you know," said Ralph.

"Look, don't listen to me, but do talk to Grace, and listen to what she has to say. I'm sure you'll work it out."

"Thanks, I'll do that. Thanks to both of you. It was all getting on top of me and I couldn't think of anyone else to ask. I knew you, Ralph would take me seriously, you always did, but thanks, Sally. I'll never be rude about librarians again." As he left, he kissed her on the cheek.

They waved him off back to London and his uncertain future. As he drove away, Sally said, "Wow, please don't ever do that to me again. I can't solve other people's problems I'm only a librarian."

"Ah yes!" said Ralph, "but you're my librarian."

"You will keep having the last word. I will have my revenge."

"You'll have to catch me first," he said and ran back into the house. Sally chased after him and caught him in the living room.

"I told you, maybe not today etc…" she paused. "Ralph, my darling, I do like being married to you."

Chapter 45

At the beginning of May, John Ashcroft rang Ralph on his mobile phone to tell him that there was a letter in the local paper which he thought they ought to see. Ralph knew that a copy of the local newspaper was held in the university library and rang Sally to ask her to look. She went into the atrium and found someone was looking at the paper. As she could not see the newspapers from the Information Desk where she was working, she kept surreptitiously strolling in that direction until the reader put down the paper and Sally whipped it away before he realised it had moved. She looked on the letter page and saw the letter.

"I am a research PhD student at Liverpool University looking into crime in Liverpool, in particularly the docks area in the aftermath of the Second World War. There were several notable incidents but I am trying to locate any living relatives of George Ashcroft of Ormsbury who might be able to tell me about him. In return, I have information that they might be interested in. Please contact me via the newspaper." *Frank Kinsella.*

"Wow," thought Sally. "This is really dynamite. A Kinsella looking for a George Ashcroft. We are really going to have to look into this."

At lunchtime, she walked into town and bought a copy of the paper and had just enough time to pass it to Ralph before her afternoon began. All afternoon, when she had a lull in her work, her thoughts drifted to the George Ashcroft/Kinsella problem and wondered what would be the best way of dealing with it. Obviously, the easiest thing to do would be to do nothing. They had found out about George's background. They had met his family and set those minds at rest as to what had happened to him. Was there any need to get more involved? She concluded that whatever they did it would be Ralph's decision and if he wanted to talk it over with Uncle John then so be it.

Ralph, meanwhile, had almost come to the same conclusion. He had waited for Sally to finish work as his timetabled lectures had finished at 3.00 pm. Thinking about the possible disadvantages that getting involved might entail, he decided to talk it over with Sally before doing anything. On the way home they both gave their thoughts on the matter and chewed it over and over again nearly all evening. Was there an ulterior motive to this Frank Kinsella? Was he as open as he appeared? Where did he fit into the Kinsella family? Was he looking to finish the job that George had run from all those years before? Was he only looking for answers as they had been? And then there was Smith's book with its accusation that the Kinsella family had murdered George and his family in revenge. Sally and Ralph knew this was not true. Was Frank Kinsella trying to correct this? They had a lot to discuss. In the end, they decided to find out more and Ralph rang John to tell him about it.

After the opening greeting, Ralph said, "Uncle John, Sally and I have discussed this letter and we think that we would like to get in touch with Frank Kinsella and try to find out what he is after. Have you any objections?"

"You must do what you think is right, lad," was the reply, "but remember the mess we got ourselves into the last time we talked to someone about this. That Smith chap who got it all wrong. Just be careful," was John's final remark.

Ralph turned to Sally, "John has no objections, just told me to be careful, so I think we'll write to Frank Kinsella and find out more. What about writing at the weekend when we've slept on it?"

"I think that sounds like one of your better ideas," replied Sally.

At the weekend they carefully wrote out a reply to send to the newspaper. It took a bit of doing as they wanted to give some information but not too much. In the end, they settled for "Dear Mr Kinsella, if you are looking for relatives of the George Ashcroft who was involved with Michael Kinsella in the Dock Road Murder, I may be able to help you. What is it exactly that you want to know?" They could have gone into more detail but wanted to get an answer first. The letter was sent in Ralph's name of Armstrong and the address given was the English Department at West Lancashire University which meant that there could be no link made directly with George Ashcroft. As the letter was sent to the newspaper and it would take some time to reach Mr Kinsella, they were not holding out too much hope of an early reply. As a result, they were surprised to receive an answer late the following week.

The reply which came from the Social Science Department at Liverpool University enlarged on Mr Kinsella's interest by explaining that he was doing a PhD thesis at Liverpool University in Social Science and was looking at post-war conditions in Liverpool which gave rise to some of the most notorious criminal activity in the city. The Kinsella murder case was one of those he was interested in and the fate of George Ashcroft, because of the uncertainty of his fate, was important. Sally and Ralph both decided that Kinsella was more than just peripherally interested in the fate of George as he had only been a minor player in the crime. Kinsella still had not explained his connection with Michael Kinsella and until he did, they decided not to give too much away.

As a result, Ralph decided to take the bull by the horns and ask directly if Frank Kinsella was related to Michael Kinsella so that if the answer was "Yes", they could act accordingly. This time the reply amazed them.

The letter came from a home address. "Dear Mr Armstrong," Frank Kinsella wrote, "I see that you have more than a passing interest in this and so I will be direct with you. Yes. Michael Kinsella was my father and although I am researching more than just my family's part in the events following the war. I am particularly interested in the fate of George Ashcroft in the light of Martin Smith's book on the subject. If you have any information as to the whereabouts of George Ashcroft, I should be delighted to hear it. My family has always strenuously denied any involvement in the disappearance of George Ashcroft. If you are willing, I should like to meet you to discuss what we know and if possible, put the record straight. Yours in anticipation, Frank Kinsella."

Both Sally and Ralph poured over the letter to see if there was anything they were missing until the paper began to look the worse for wear.

"I think we are going to have to meet him," Ralph said for the umpteenth time. "I think he genuinely wants to know what happened to George. What do you think?"

"I think that you're right," agreed Sally, "but I think we ought to meet on neutral ground. What about the Adelphi Hotel in Liverpool? We could get there by train so wouldn't need to worry about parking. Also, it's not far from the University."

So Ralph replied. This time he put their home address on the letter as a sign of good faith. He suggested the following Saturday afternoon at the Adelphi at 2.00 pm and added his mobile phone number as an additional sign of good faith. Two days later Frank rang to say he would be at the Adelphi so they both looked forward to the weekend with a little hint of apprehension.

Chapter 46

The late Spring in May was beginning to turn into a hot and sultry summer when Sally and Ralph set off to meet Frank Kinsella. Ralph decided to take some photographs, to show Mr Kinsella, which might help to confirm the identity of George. Both he and Sally were convinced by now that they and Kinsella were talking about the same person. But if Frank had photographs of George with Michael, then an identification would be possible. The train journey into Liverpool passed without a hitch and the short walk from Central Station to the Hotel was made through a hot and sticky afternoon and they were relieved to walk into the cool dark foyer of the hotel.

They looked around for the lounge. As they entered, they saw an elderly man sitting alone at one of the tables and made their way over to him. As they approached, he stood up in welcome and held out his hand to Ralph.

"Mr Armstrong, I presume," he said. "Do you know, I've always wanted to say that?"

"You presume correctly," replied Ralph taking the proffered hand. "This is my wife, Sally." Frank shook hands with Sally. "She has been helping me," Ralph continued, "– in fact, that is totally wrong, she has been doing all the work and I've been hindering her. She's my 'family history' guru who has tracked all the information down, so I have brought her along to hear what I hope is the end of the story."

"Well. I am very pleased to meet you both. I hope that when we have finished talking, we will both have heard something that will please us," said Frank Kinsella.

They ordered pots of tea and cakes and before they came the conversation started.

"Perhaps," said Ralph, "you wouldn't mind explaining why you want to know about George Ashcroft."

"Not at all," Frank replied. "As I told you in my letter Michael Kinsella was my father and I knew George Ashcroft when I was a small boy. I have fond memories of him as sometimes he was like a big kid himself. As you know my father instigated a robbery on the Dock Road during which a policeman was shot and killed. George Ashcroft gave evidence at the trial and subsequently disappeared. That has troubled me. As I say I knew him. I never thought too much about it until Martin Smith's book came out and resurrected all the old memories. When it was suggested, no, not suggested, given as a definite statement of fact, that my father was instrumental in his disappearance I was mortified. Was the past ever going to be put to rest? Would we ever escape from it? By this time my mother had died and I could no longer ask her any questions. She had, however, left some papers and I had a look through them and what I found led me to do my thesis."

"Before we go any further do you have a photograph of the George Ashcroft you knew. If we can compare it with one of my grandfather's, will know if we are talking about the same person," said Ralph.

"As a matter of fact I have got just one with George on," answered Frank. "It was taken when George drove us to the seaside at Rhyl." He produced an enlargement of a photograph showing a smiling family group of a mother and father and two young boys with an extra man standing at the side. "That's George," he said.

Ralph reached into his briefcase and produced an enlargement of the one family group that he had of his grandparents with his father taken in the garden of their home in Cleckheaton. He passed it across to Frank who compared it with his photograph. He then passed them both to Sally and Ralph who studied them again, and then Sally compared them side by side.

"I think they are of the same person," she said. "Obviously, in this one of yours," she said to Frank, "he is much younger. But I'm pretty certain, they are the same person." She gave both photographs to Frank who looked at them and then handed them to Ralph. Ralph looked at them both and said, "You're right, they are the same person."

Frank looked pleased, and said, "I agree. This is a great load off my mind. Now I can prove that my father had nothing to do with George's disappearance."

"Actually," said Ralph, "I don't think you can say that."

"Why?" asked Frank.

"Two days after Michael Kinsella shouted from the dock, that he knew where George lived, and that he would suffer for what he had done. George's parents were killed in an accident and George took fright and left Ormsbury with his own family. He left his relatives and the district and never got in touch with any of them ever again. He left his identity behind and became someone else. So I think I could argue that your father did have something to do with George's disappearance."

"I see your point. But certainly, my father definitely didn't have him killed."

"That is true," agreed Ralph.

"Well that is a relief to me," said Frank, "as I always wondered, at least ever since Smith's book. Now tell me. How do you come to have this photograph?"

"It's quite simple really," said Ralph. "George Ashcroft was my grandfather, his son, John, was my father."

"I remember a baby," said Frank. "George must have brought him to show my mother not long after he was born. There was a lady with him."

"That would be my grandmother."

"But your name is Armstrong, not Ashcroft."

"That's another consequence of your father's outburst," said Ralph. "He changed his name as well as cutting himself off from everything and everyone he had ever known." Ralph was beginning to get angry on his grandfather's behalf. "He always said, and drummed it into my father's head, that under no circumstances was any member of the family to ever go to Ormsbury. We only found out last year, when I asked Sally to help me find out why, that his name was really Ashcroft. As a result, I have only recently found a whole new family whom I knew nothing about."

Frank sat in silence for a while. "I am truly sorry," he said. "I had no idea that it had caused all this trouble. I was only seeing it from my family's point of view. I thought that if I could exonerate my father from an additional murder then I could live with the one I knew about. But I can see that for you it has been a lifelong curse."

They all sat in silence for a while. Frank reached for the plate of cakes and handed them round. He ordered a fresh pot of tea.

"Let me tell you what I know about your grandfather. See if it fits in with what you have found out."

"I should like that," said Ralph. "I never knew him, you know, he died when my father was about twelve."

"I'm sorry to hear that," said Frank. "I'm afraid my family has been the source of a great deal of anguish over the years." After a pause, he continued, "Some of this I found out later from my uncle Brian and my mother and some of it I got from unpublished police material when I started researching for my thesis. Because it was so long ago and because of my interest the police have been very helpful. I have known nearly all my life that my father was a criminal. I did not find out that he had been hanged for murder until much later when another boy at school told me. My mother always told me that he had died, but not how, or even when. After I left school, I did several jobs and then decided to become a probation officer. I thought that if my father had been a criminal and I could not save him, I ought at least to try to rescue others. I retired from that about five years ago and thought I would do some research to fill my time and began to wonder about Liverpool after the war and to try to understand the kind of person my father was. I sometimes wonder what he would have turned out like if he hadn't decided to go in for armed robbery.

"One of my earliest memories is of a party in a pub somewhere, my mother said later that it was to celebrate him getting out of prison. He had been involved in the black market during the war. Mother said, he had too much charm and was very charismatic. He drew people towards him. She felt it but knew it was dangerous. She tried to shield both of us boys from it as much as possible. I sometimes think she was glad he went because it meant that we didn't get sucked into his way of life and ended up in gaol. She wanted us to go straight, as did his mother my grandmother. She did not approve of my father. I don't know whether it was at that party that your grandfather first met Pa but it must have been soon after because I remember him from that far back."

"John, George's brother, said that George loved going to the gangster films at the cinema. He seemed to think there was a glamour there that was lacking in his own life," said Ralph.

"Well if he was looking for glamour, he wouldn't need to go further than Pa," replied Frank. "He had glamour enough lots of parties and plenty to eat. When I think about it now, it must have all been black market stuff because there was still rationing. Anyway, George got drawn into Pa's circle. He was good with cars. That's how I remember him mostly, driving us to school or to the coast. Ma liked him. We had a big car, I remember. I think it was American."

"Aunt Lily remembered that. He must have borrowed it one day and took it up to Ormsbury because she sat in the front seat when George took it round the block. She had never seen anything like it."

"I'd never seen anything like before or since, God knows where Pa got it from. Anyway, George was a very good mechanic and could tune an engine to a T. So when Pa wanted a fast car and a driver, he knew whom to ask. I'm pretty certain George had never been involved in any of Pa's schemes until that last one. Ma said Pa was trying to up his status and get into the big league by trying to get into a drugs racket. Up to then, he had been small time. He could have gone legitimate at the end of rationing if he'd wanted to work, but Ma said he liked the thrill of the risk. So he would probably have ended up badly eventually. You've read about the trial?" Ralph nodded. "Well, you know it all went wrong. It had been a police set up to catch the drugs ring, and Pa got caught in the middle of it with a gun which went off and killed a policeman. There was no doubt that it was Pa's gun that did it. There were no other shots and no other guns were found. George drove off but they were caught with the gun which had Pa's fingerprints on it. George was terrified, mind you Pa was terrified too, he didn't realise that it was loaded. Which just shows you that he was never going to make it in the big league. George turned King's evidence, or Queen's evidence by the time it came to court. The trial only lasted four days. Brian got ten years but Pa got a death sentence. Ma took us to Ireland so we didn't know what was going on. She came back for the trial and saw him in Walton gaol. He wrote to her. She asked him about George. He swore on his mother's life that he had had nothing to do with George's disappearance. She believed him. What happened from your side?"

Ralph took up the story. "Two days after the trial George's parents were coming home from an evening out visiting friends. They were standing at a bus stop in Maghull when a car ploughed into them killing them both. George thought, at least this is what we have worked out, that it was an indirect attempt on his life for turning Queen's evidence and he ran, changed his name and settled in an out of the way place where he thought no one would ever find him. He drove a trolley bus in Bradford, he never let on he was a mechanic. Dad said that he would get someone else to mend his bicycle. He was killed in an accident on the trolley bus. I suppose it was a bit ironic. By the time I was born we were Armstrongs, Dad never said anything different. It was only when Sally and I, started looking into this that we found out his real name. Dad always said his father said "Never go to Ormsbury, but of course, I'm the awkward one who always does the opposite to what I'm told to do. Sally will confirm that." He smiled at Sally who smiled back.

Sally had sat for the whole afternoon silently listening to all that was said. It wasn't her family and apart from her love for Ralph it was the family history side of the story that interested her. Ralph took her hand. "Do you know, love," he said, "I think we have finally reached the end of the story." He turned to Frank,

"Thank you," he said, "having heard your side of the story and heard it from the Ashcrofts I feel that I now know where I come from and where I fit in. I can tell my sister that there is nothing to fear and I can tell her all about it now. Thank you again."

Chapter 47

The anniversary of the Orphans' Picnic came round again and Ralph and Sally repeated their picnic of the previous year. This time next year they would be living in Yorkshire so they looked on it as the time of saying goodbye to Ormsbury. The weather was fine and bright and even warm, and after eating they strolled along the ridge of Ashurst Beacon with its view of Winter Hill and the distant Pennines. Ralph told Sally that he had received a letter from Tom saying that he had had a serious conversation with Grace and he had high hopes for the future. Ralph had not let Sally read the letter as Tom had made some very complimentary remarks about Sally and derogatory remarks about him, and he had not wanted her to get a big head.

It was later that night after they had gone to bed when Ralph started considering what had happened during the year. They had retired to bed early and Ralph made gentle love to Sally and she responded. Afterwards, they lay comfortably together and dozed and drowsed for some time until Ralph's brain clicked into gear.

"I've just been thinking over what has happened over the last two years," said Ralph. "I mean, two years ago I took a risk and disobeyed all that Dad ever told me which was 'Never go to Ormsbury son, something bad might happen'. I got a two-year post not really expecting anything would happen. Ria was so cross with me. But I came anyway. Not only that but once here I decided to try to solve the mystery which seemed to have haunted Dad. I must have needed my head examined. What happened? It has been a fantastic couple of years. First, I found you, then I got married, and then together we found out why my grandfather never wanted us to come back here. Do you know it has all been worthwhile and I don't regret any of it?"

"Neither do I," replied Sally. "Meeting you was the best thing though."

"I suppose you are going to add that you knew I needed my head examining."

"No, I just thought that you were the nicest new member of staff we had had for a long time."

"When did you realise that?"

"When I told you, I might have to kill you, if I explained the Dewey Classification System to you. I knew it was a daft thing to say, but you laughed and I knew that you were the one for me. I always wanted someone whom I could make laugh, and not take me or things too seriously. When did you know about me?"

"At about the same time. You brought a lightness to the whole thing which I found refreshing. Most Librarians seem to take their work so seriously."

"I do take things seriously, you know, but only the important things," said Sally. "The incidental things are fun, silly, something to laugh at. I've always felt that life was for laughing at, only people were for serious consideration!!!"

"So it has all worked out well for you too?"

"Oh! I think so. You're right. It has been a fantastic couple of years, and I would not change a thing. I'm now looking forward, to York and all that it will bring."

"Me too. That's very complimentary assuming I'm part of it. But how do you mean?"

"You have brought an added dimension to my life that I never thought to have. Do you know," she added, "none of this would have happened if I had gone out with you all those years ago in Leeds."

"How do you mean?"

"Well, let's assume that we had got on and ultimately got married."

"Right," said Ralph cautiously.

"We would probably be living in a university town somewhere, you would never have had the incentive to come to Ormsbury because you would be so content with me, and you would have put the problem to the back of your mind."

'This woman has a very inflated idea of herself,' thought Ralph.

"What I am saying is that you would not have solved the mystery, and by the time our children started looking, all the people we have been talking to would no longer be with us. You would still not know why you were not supposed to ever come to Ormsbury and we would not have got an answer. You would not have acquired a whole new set of relatives who in turn would still be wondering what had happened to brother George, and you would have never learned the truth. Mr Kinsella would still not know that his father had not had George murdered as that silly book said. So this has just been the right time."

"That's true. You're right. I probably wouldn't have had any incentive to come to find out. I suppose I might have come on a day trip to see what all the fuss was about, and what would I have found? Nothing but a quiet market town where nothing ever happens and would have learnt nothing."

"And I would never have been here either to get involved with family history and be able to help you answer the question."

"So what are you saying?"

"I'm thinking that your long greasy hair served its purpose and brought us together at exactly the right time to solve the mystery, and answer all the questions."

"Are you actually suggesting that you are glad that we did not get together all those years ago?"

"No. I am saying that because we didn't, ghosts have been laid to rest, the truth is out and the truth has set us/you free to enjoy the rest of our lives."

Ralph lay back in bed and looked at the ceiling, "I was just regretting the lost years," he said, "but you're right, as usual, I would still not have known. I was rather a pain at times, not being able to relax. I did wonder sometimes why it concerned me so because it did. It definitely bothered Dad and it must have rubbed off on me. Maybe," he pondered, "he brought me up to be the man of the family who needed to slay the dragons and, in this instance, I did not even know where the dragons were."

"Maybe the dragon that you were looking for, was the truth. Come on, Literary Expert, who was it who said, 'There is nothing to fear except fear itself?'"

"I forget, but you're right. I saw a chance and came here for answers, and thanks to you I found them. So we can now go forward. York, here we come."

"I think so. You're right. It has been a fantastic couple of years, and I would not change a thing. So now, as I said, I'm looking forward, to York."

Just before she dropped off to sleep Sally said, "I'm going to write the story of George and what happened to him and put the record straight. We cannot let that silly book be the last word on George."

Epilogue

"Dear Sir," Sally wrote, "some time ago you published a book called *Murder on the Dock Road and other Mysteries* by Martin Smith. In this, the author accused the Kinsella gang of murdering George Ashcroft, one of the witnesses against Michael Kinsella at his trial. I understand that Martin Smith had since died and so I cannot tell him the following story. However, I enclose a copy for your information. I retain copyright on it as does Mr Frank Kinsella who also knows the whole truth. Yours faithfully…"

THE STORY OF GEORGE ASHCROFT

In the middle 1940s, George Ashcroft left school at the age of 15 and got an apprenticeship as a motor mechanic. He was not academically bright but was good with his hands and he enjoyed the work and the camaraderie of his workmates. Having now left school he had the time and a little money to explore the world, a world which had been left in tatters after the Second World War. He discovered the cinema and spent a good deal of his spare time locked in the embrace of the silver screen. He started out following westerns where men were men and women liked them that way. The law was what you wanted it to be and it came out of the barrel of a gun. Later he developed a taste for gangster movies these reflected the aftermath of the war with the sleazy glamour of spivs and their molls. He adopted a greasy, slicked back hairstyle, carried a wooden pistol in his coat pocket ready to tackle any opposition and walked with a rolling gait which indicated that he was not a man to be messed with. His friends thought it was harmless showing off and he knew that it was all fantasy. But what he craved was the reality.

Ormsbury was a small town with only two secondary schools so that everybody knew everybody and no one had any secrets. It had, however, one advantage. It was linked by public transport to the potentially glamorous attractions of Liverpool with its promise of anonymity where he could potentially act out his fantasy for real. As a result, one fateful Saturday, he took the train into Liverpool to look for what his heart craved. As luck would have it, he chose the exact day and almost the time to walk into the Golden Lion pub on the corner of London Road, when Michael Kinsella returned from a two-year stretch in Durham Gaol.

George had strolled into the pub using his acquired rolling gait and his pseudo air of 'Don't mess with me' to find himself almost immediately included in a celebratory party for the hero's return. Michael was in a good mood. He was in his late twenties, of middle height, handsome and with an easy charm and charisma which drew people to him. He was also a spiv who had made money selling stolen, as well as forged petrol coupons and anything else anyone wanted. He did not use violence but boasted a host of contacts who could get anything for anybody if the price was right. Some of the goods were stolen, some faked, but if anyone complained he obligingly gave them their money back, with no hard feelings. He knew they would be back for something else. All this activity brought him to the attention of the police but his charm and lack of people to testify against him meant that, if caught, he was sent down on minor charges and it was his release from one of these that he was celebrating on that Saturday night.

For George this was glamour, this was what he wanted to be, for once in his short life he had stumbled, accidentally, onto the 'real thing'. Michael had noticed him straight away. A stranger at a party meant they were either an innocent or a police spy so he made it his business to find out more and engaged George in conversation. It did not take him long to find out what an innocent George was. George was only too eager to tell this charming man all about himself, where he came from and of his talent with car engines. Later Michael was never quite sure why he thought that George could be of use to him. All men had their uses as far as Michael was concerned. But he also realised that in the two years he had been out of circulation the world was changing. Rationing, that mainstay of the spiv, was coming to an end. If he wanted to maintain his lifestyle and support his wife and two young children, he would have to find alternative sources of income and just at the moment, he was uncertain in which direction to go. But somewhere at the back of his head was the thought that a man who could do things with cars could be a very useful person to know.

Michael belonged to a large extended family of men on the make, and women who worried about them. He had married young, 'to keep him out of mischief' as his mother put it, but the arrival, in short order, of two boys meant that money was tight and his record meant that legitimate employment was beyond his grasp even if he had wanted it. It was much more fun being on the fly. Life was fun for Michael.

To George, all this attention was like manna from heaven. By the end of the evening, he would have died for Michael if he had asked him to. On the train back to Ormsbury he re-ran the evening in his mind and was convinced that he had a future as an aide in this glamorous world. On his first night of venture out of his normal world, he had been shown something new and exciting. What he was actually getting himself into, he had no idea.

All the following week, he looked forward to going back into Liverpool on Saturday and tried to imagine what kind of reception he would get when he went back to the Golden Lion. When Saturday night finally came and he entered the pub all was quiet. Only a few regulars were drinking and playing dominoes. Michael was not there, neither was any of the crowd that had been there the previous Saturday. His disappointment was almost tangible. That was until the barman said, "Are you George?" When he replied that he was, the barman handed him a note. It was from Michael. The note read: "Sorry not to see you on Saturday but I have other plans. I enjoyed meeting you last week will be in touch." To George, this was almost an invitation to heaven. He did not appreciate that it could also have more sinister undertones from a man like Michael Kinsella. George had a pint of beer and decided to go home, there was no glamour that night.

Every Saturday night, over the next few weeks he presented himself at the Golden Lion, and most Saturdays there was a message from Michael. He did not realise that he was being kept on hold until Michael had a little job for him to do. As a result, the message from Michael came to be almost as important to George as an actual meeting. Then, glory be, one Saturday there was Michael waiting for him when he went into the Golden Lion.

"I've been waiting for you," he said. "I've got a job for you. By now you should have finished that apprenticeship of yours, have you?"

"Yes," said George.

"Righty Ho," replied Michael, "I've bought a nice little car and I want you to look after it. When can you start?"

"Week on Monday," said George, "I'll have to give notice." Michael laughed.

"You're a good little boy then, always doing things by the book. I like that. It shows that you can be trusted." George was flattered. "If this goes well, I'm looking to buy a bigger car, and you will help me chose it." George did not know what to say.

From the day George started working for Michael he thought he was in seventh heaven. The car he looked after was a sporty little number that Michael used to show off in. He also had another car which his wife and children used and gradually George took over caring for that as well. Kitty Kinsella did not drive and George became the chauffeur for the family.

Over the next two or three years, he became an accepted part of the Kinsella clan. During this period, he acquired a girlfriend, all glamorous gangsters have a-moll, and in short order a wife and son. George's idea of birth control was a little hazy, to say the least and his mother did not have the same philosophy as Michael's in finding him a wife 'to keep him out of trouble' and into trouble George got. Poor Elizabeth Grimshaw, 'Betty', one minute she was a hairdresser and the next a wife and mother with a husband she hardly knew and whom she hardly ever saw as he worked in Liverpool for a mysterious businessman and she lived in Ormsbury with her mother.

Throughout the whole of this period, George was not in any trouble. He worked for Michael. What Michael did was of no concern to him. Michael also kept out of the arms of the law, but not out of their ken. The police kept their eye on him, but as to all intents and purposes, he was an honest businessman who they could not touch. Perhaps after all his youthful criminality, he had finally decided to go straight.

He had his finger in many pies, property, letting substandard accommodation to immigrants, bookmaking both legal and illegal, managing entertainment groups, anything that would bring in ostensibly honest earnings but which could cover for illegal earnings as well. He had learned his early lessons well. That is until one of his brothers brought him a juicy bit of gossip. A ship was bringing in a big supply of drugs. Up to now, Michael had kept well clear of drug dealing, he knew it went on, he knew who was behind it and he knew it was big business, but he had kept his hands clean. This, however, looked like too good an opportunity to miss. If he could get his hands on it, he knew the dealers, he could pass the drugs on with minimal risk to himself, and had the prospect of making a killing and moving up into the big time.

To do the job properly he needed a van, a beat-up old van, which looked as though it went at a crawl but had power under the bonnet. This is when he realised what a prize he had caught in George. He sent George out to buy the oldest, but soundest van he could get, and to soup up the engine until it purred like a cat and could outrun any police car or sports car in the district. George bought the van and realised that if Michael wanted speed, he would have to fit a new engine. As the potential prize was so great Michael readily agreed to the expense and George fitted the engine and tuned it to perfection.

Michael's plan, such as it was, was a smash and grab affair. His plan was to locate the drugs, grab them and outrun any chasing dealers or police and hide the van in a lock-up until the hue and cry died down. To deter any interference, he was going to use guns. This was the first time he had ever used guns in any of his activities and while he thought he knew the risks he also thought he was in control.

It was all organized. The shipment of drugs was to arrive on Thursday at the Gladstone dock. It would be brought ashore by one of the dockers in his lunch pail. He had been identified by Brian Kinsella who would be in the car with Michael at the point where he was to be stopped. George was to drive the van.

The van was parked a short distance away from the dock gates and as the docker walked home they would grab him put him in the van and drive off at speed. They would relieve him of the drugs and push him out as they slowed at the crossroads.

The van would then drive into the lock-up garage and they would separate until the heat had died down. Only later would they try to offload the drugs.

What they did not know was that it was a sting operation run by the Drug Squad to catch the real drug dealers in the act. The docker was actually an undercover policeman. All went according to plan until the docker was captured. This was where the scheme fell down. They had forgotten to put masks on and it was obvious that the docker would recognise them again and Michael shot him before pushing him out of the back of the van at speed. The policeman died.

As the whole incident had taken place under the police's nose, they knew precisely who had tried to steal the drugs and Michael, Brian and George were arrested before the end of the day. Michael and Brian stuck to their story that they did not know the gun was loaded and that it must have gone off accidentally, but George was scared, this was going too far even for his fevered imagination and he told the police that it was Michael who had fired the shot. On the basis of George's statement and the fingerprint evidence, Michael was charged with murder.

George was terrified that he would also be charged with murder and so turned Queen's evidence at the trial. Following the trial when Michael Kinsella shouted from the dock, that he knew where George lived. Following the subsequent death of his parents in a car accident, George gathered his wife and child and a few mementoes and fled from Ormsbury never to be seen there again.

However, he went to Cleckheaton in Yorkshire, changed his name, and made a new life for himself and his family. He died in 1962 and his son in 2003. But he had a grandson who was always told never to go to Ormsbury. He, Ralph, being an Ashcroft and up for an adventure, went to Ormsbury to find out why. The answer is the story you have just read.